The Other Side of the Ledge

THE OTHER SIDE OF THE LEDGE

by

Janelle Parmer

ISBN: 9798692099815 (paperback)

Thanks to my family and friends who helped make this book possible. Without their love, encouragement, and support, this would still just be an idea floating around in my head.

A special thank you to my parents, who were the first ones that read the original draft of *The Other Side of the Ledge*, and gave me feedback along the way. Thanks to my sister, Liz, who continued to tell me to keep writing and it will all work out.

In addition, a special thanks to my husband, Mike, who encouraged me and loved me throughout the process. Even when I was writing at all hours of the night, or the entire weekend was me spent on the computer, trying to edit a chapter, he didn't complain at all. He told me to keep writing and was the driving force for me to finish this incredible project that I started over a decade ago.

Mental health is an important topic that we are now just starting to scratch the surface on. My goal is that *The Other Side of the Ledge* will continue to inspire these crucial conversations.

I hope you enjoy reading *The Other Side of the Ledge*, as much as I enjoyed writing it. Happy reading!

CHAPTER 1

"Kara, Kara!"

I heard shouting in the house. I leaped out of bed and ran to the top of the stairs. "Chris, Chris!" I pleaded, but only found Beth walking up the staircase toward me.

"Where the hell have you been? Sleeping all day?" Beth asked, even though she already knew the answer.

"No, I was just taking a nap, that's all."

"A nap?" Beth asked as she looked me up and down. "You're still wearing your sweats. You never even got dressed today, did you?"

"What day is it?" I asked innocently.

"It's Thursday, Kara. You promised you would go tonight, remember?"

"Thursday already. Wow, I thought we just had Thursday not too long ago."

"We did. Last week," Beth squawked.

"You look horrible," I lied.

"What do you mean I look horrible? You're the one

who hasn't eaten or showered in days, let alone gotten dressed."

"I know I look horrible, but what's your excuse?"

"Must be hereditary then," Beth quipped back.

"I'm just kidding. You look great as always." And she did. Beth was four years younger than I, two sizes bigger, and looked beautiful as usual. We were both around five-foot-five, but always fought over who was actually the taller one. She stood next to me when Chris and I got married. I repaid the favor of being her matron of honor when she got married. Beth and Mark practically got pregnant on their honeymoon and had three-year-old twin boys, Ben and Elijah. Mark was good to her and worked as a pilot for a major airline. They were perfect together. Like Chris and I were perfect together.

"I just said that because I knew you were going to say I look horrible, and I wanted to beat you to it."

"Very competitive of you." Beth half smiled.

"It's about all I have left," I said, half joking, half holding back tears.

"Get over here, you stick." Beth smiled, holding back tears of her own as she hugged me intensely. "Now get your ass in that shower, or I'm gonna drag you into the front yard, and hose you down myself."

"Wow, wonder what the neighbors would say then?" I smirked.

"I bet they would thank me and give me a standing ovation."

"Ha ha," I said as I returned to the bedroom and walked into the master bathroom. Beth followed, probably making sure I wasn't just going to turn the water on, sit next to the tub sobbing, wait fifteen minutes, roll my hair in a towel, and thank her for making me take a shower because I felt so much better now. She had recently caught on to this and now was a prison warden to my personal hygiene. God, I wished she would just leave me alone.

I turned the water on high, tossed my clothes off, and jumped in the shower. Beth started to giggle.

"What's so damn funny?" I asked.

"Oh, nothing. I was just thinking I have probably seen you naked more in the past month than in your whole life put together." Beth giggled again.

"Well, I'm glad you're enjoying yourself," I murmured.

"What did you say?"

"Nothing."

The warm water did feel nice over my skin, and washing my hair felt even better, but I didn't know why I was cleaning myself. I lived alone. No one to share my meals, my bed, or my love with anymore.

"Hey, come on, it's five thirty already!" Beth shouted from my bedroom.

"So what? You want me clean. I'm getting clean!" I shouted back.

Beth walked into the bathroom. "The meeting starts at six thirty."

"What meeting?" I asked.

"Don't play cutsie with me. You know what meeting. The meeting you have been avoiding. Tonight, you are going."

"I don't think I'm ready yet."

"Ready yet for what? I'm not asking you to go lead a goddamn parade, Kara. Just go sit in a room with a bunch of people. That's all."

"No, that's not it. I have to go sit and talk about it, and I don't want to. It's done. I'm here, he's dead, and that's that. End of story."

"No, that's not the end of the story. You need to deal with what happened so you can get on with your life."

I shut the water off and grabbed a towel as I stepped out of the shower.

"Get on with my life? What life? Chris was my life, and now he's dead. Dead! There is nothing else I want out of life. Life has nothing more to offer."

"I hate it when you talk like that. Please stop. You're only thirty-seven years old. You have much more time to explore life."

"I don't want to *explore* life. It's been explored. I have nothing more to add to it. There are what, seven billion people in the world? Let them explore it while I sleep."

"Kare, listen to me." Beth grabbed my shoulders. "You promised you would do this. If not for me, yourself, or Mom, then for Chris. He wouldn't want to see you like this."

"Well, I don't think Chris really thought that far in advance, now did he?"

I returned to the bedroom and saw Beth had already laid my clothes out on the bed. Black slacks with a brown sweater. Brown to match Chris's eyes, I would have told him. Beth finished getting me ready, pushed me out the front door, and we climbed into her minivan. This was what Beth must have felt like when I was in high school being her chauffeur. Beth wove in and out of traffic like a California pro. "What's the hurry?" I asked. "Tired of my delightful company already?"

"No." She smirked. "Just don't want you to be late for your first meeting, that's all."

"I'm sure it will be okay as long as you write me a note."

It was completely dark outside. Spring would be here soon, and it would be time to change the clocks again. Right now, I could have just stayed in the dark all of the time and not cared a bit. I was loathing spring this year. Spring just meant summer would be next. Chris had been an English professor at the local university and always used the summers to focus on his personal work. He was my house husband from the end of June till August. Most summer nights, I would come home from my job as a paralegal, and he would already have dinner started and the table set on the patio. Those long, lovely summer evenings were magical. We would often sit out on the back patio, relax, eat, and talk about his day of writing and research, or my day at the office. I had always dreaded the beginning of fall. It meant classes were once again in session, Chris would return to working and researching fifty to sixty hours per week, and I would come home to an empty house. Little did I know then that I would soon be living in the fall season for the rest of my life.

The minivan came to a sudden stop.

"Do you want me to come in with you?" Beth asked.

"No, I think I can manage."

"I know you can manage; I just meant for support."

"I guess you don't remember how embarrassing it is for kids to have their parents come to class with them," I said as I rolled my eyes.

"Stop, you know what I mean."

"I know, you can make it up to me by taking me for ice cream now."

"After class…if you're a good girl."

"Define good," I said.

"Stay for the entire class, and don't say anything too mean."

"Darn, that's a lot to ask."

"Oh, and…"

"That's quite enough. See you at eight."

"See you." Beth kissed me on the cheek. "I love you, you know," she said softly.

"Love you too." I rushed out of the minivan and shut the door. If you love me, I thought, then why are you kidnapping and making me go here?

Oh, to be on a high school campus again. Butterflies flew in my stomach just like they had on my first day of classes. Back then I'd spent so much time worrying how I looked; if I saw myself now, I would have dropped out of school. Damp hair, no makeup, and red eyes. Guess I'll have a lot more trouble getting asked to the prom this time around.

I pulled a small slip of paper from my pocket. "Room 238," I whispered to myself. I saw a class with lights on across the quad area. That was probably it. I deliberately walked a leisurely pace and still arrived at the staircase too soon. I slowly began my ascent up the steep stairs. Maybe this whole thing was a metaphor for life. We have to start our journey at the bottom, and then we eventually get to the light, our purpose. Nah, psychobabble crap. I bet the shrink running this group thought of that when they saw the classroom for the first time. I finally made it to the top of the stairs and noticed a long row of classrooms. The room at the end of the hall had its door wide open, and the fluorescent lights blazed like an inferno all the way from back here. I couldn't see the number on the door, but there was a large sign that read "COPE Meeting."

The smell of strong coffee and store-bought cookies filled the air. I thought I had planned everything perfectly and would have entered the class about two minutes after it had begun. I was supposed to come in, see everyone already seated, and then quickly sneak a seat in the back. They would already be so immersed in their own stories of grief and coping strategies that they wouldn't even notice me enter the room. I would sit, pretending to listen for an hour or so, and slither out just as they were closing the session. My detention would be over, I would rush to the ridiculous minivan, and Beth would drive me to get ice cream. I could do this. My plan was perfect, except for one fatal flaw: the class obviously didn't start on time. It was 7:05 p.m., and people were still standing around the refreshment table and mingling in corners of the room, and a few were still arranging chairs into a circle—a circle, another flaw in my plan. How could I hide in a friggin' circle? My plan was being defeated even before it began. I felt exhausted already.

"Hi, my name's Jan. You must be new. I don't remember seeing you before. What's your name?"

Oh crap, it had already begun. "Kara," I muttered under my breath, reaching out to meet her perky, unwanted hand.

"Don't worry, Kara, we won't bite…at least not at the first meeting." Jan laughed a reprehensible, self-pleasing laugh. I tried to smile but wasn't sure if it was working or not.

"Who's your new friend, Jan?" a faint voice asked behind me. I turned and didn't see anyone at first. Just as I was starting to turn away, I heard the same voice say, "My name is Elliot." I glanced down and saw Elliot. He was probably five feet with shoes on, if that. Elliot looked to be in his mid-forties, dressed in a nice button-down checkered shirt and khaki pants.

"Oh, hi, my name is Kara."

"Welcome. We are glad to have you," Elliot said as he made his way to one of the seats in the circle.

"Isn't he sweet?" Jan asked. "He has such a positive attitude about life." She smiled blankly in Elliot's direction.

"Well, why is he here then?" I asked.

Jan turned and glared at me as if I had just cut the hair off her favorite Barbie doll. "I'm going to grab some coffee. Do you want some?" she asked in a not-so-perky tone.

"No, thanks." I reminded myself to be nice.

Minutes felt like years. As I made my way to one of the empty seats, away from as many people as possible, I was stopped by three more people who introduced themselves and asked my name. Damn, didn't we do introductions at the beginning of the meeting, and that was it? I felt bad that I was wasting these people's time and effort to remember my name when this would be the first and last time I'd ever see them. I would be forgotten pretty quickly anyway. Maybe Jan or Elliot would ask at the next meeting if anyone had heard from me. Everyone would shake their heads no. By the following meeting, I would be completely forgotten, and they were bound to have a new recruit whose name would replace mine.

"All righty then, let's get started," I heard as I sat down and looked around the circle. Who had said that? "Okay, some quick official business before we begin our meeting. We need to remember to not only put the chairs away, but the tables as well after the meeting. And bowling last week was fun, right? Well, we just need to make sure we organize carpools better next time because..." I watched the leader, the board-certified psychologist or whatever he was who was assigned to this group of losers, intently. I couldn't believe it. He looked to be maybe twenty-six years old, if that. He had his doctorate? How was that possible? He looked so young. What the hell did he know about death? Just what he had read in books and journals. Did those books tell you how to cure grief? I found myself getting angrier as I listened to him drone on about carpooling schedules and organizing a possible event next month.

"So, I see we have a few new faces in the crowd tonight. Let's have some quick introductions first. Everyone, I'm Dr. Michael Lee. I prefer to be called Mike; some people call me Dr. Mike, so it's whatever you feel comfortable with. This is our COPE group, where we talk about the grief we have experienced and continue to experience. We also talk about techniques that we have found helpful to aid us in turning our grief into positive memories and efforts in our community. Let's start over here. Please state your name and something you like to do, or someplace you would like to visit. Doesn't matter, just something fun."

"My name is Frank, and I love good food."

"Yeah, Frank is addicted to Mary's homemade cookies," the guy next to Frank said and smiled at Frank. Everyone laughed.

"It's true. I have a sweet tooth." Frank laughed.

The man next to Frank said, "My name is Efrain, and I like poetry."

"Jensen, and I would like to visit New York someday."

"I'm Georgia, and I have three beautiful children."

"Layla, and I play in a band."

"I'm Monique, and I like to shop."

"Elliot, and I would like to be an astronaut." The group lovingly laughed again.

"I'm Jan, and I love baseball."

"I'm Mary, and I would like to see my son graduate."

"Claudia, and my favorite holiday is Halloween."

"You talkin' to me? Are you talkin' to me?" said an older man wearing a checkered bow tie and holding a cane, doing a not-so-bad impersonation of Robert DeNiro. The class cracked up.

"Sal, yes, we are talkin' to you," Mike said sweetly as if talking to his own grandfather.

"I know, I know. Everyone, I'm Sal. I enjoy movies and the ladies." The group laughed again. "More importantly, I enjoy looking at ladies in the movies."

"Sal, you're gonna give yourself a heart attack talking like that," the man next to Sal said affectionately as he tapped Sal on the shoulder.

"You're just jealous because the ladies like me better!"

"You're damn right I'm jealous. The ladies my age all want a dirty old man to take care of them instead of a young stud like me who can satisfy them." The young man grinned.

"Ah, you are in a world of hurt then because I can take care of them *and* satisfy them." Sal smirked.

"All right, all right. Hi, everyone. My name is Ruben, and I would love to go to Spain someday."

"Ahhh, the senoritas in Spain. Sounds good to me. Sign me up!" Sal smiled.

"My name is Lynn, and I don't like movies. They are trash, and I prefer to read."

Sal and Ruben both rolled their eyes.

I felt everyone's eyes shift over to me. I hadn't had this many people stare at me all at one time since Chris's funeral. The temperature in the room felt like it had jumped to a hundred degrees in a matter of seconds. Say something, I told myself. Say anything to make them stop looking and move on with this stupid meeting.

"I'm Kara, and I don't watch movies or read. I like to graffiti on abandoned buildings and steal cars in my free time."

The room fell completely silent. A short laugh echoed in the room. It was Ruben.

"Excuse me?" Mike asked.

"Nothing," I answered, feeling my face and neck turn bright red. "My name is Kara, and I have three nephews and one niece."

The meeting droned on. I faded in and out of listening. The end part of my plan worked. The close of the meeting began, and I was out of there like a flash of lightning. I wanted to get out of here before fake Dr. Mike had a chance to pull me aside and analyze my awkward behavior. I needed to leave before I made empty promises about seeing everyone at the next meeting in two weeks, and how I was looking forward to joining the next bowling party. My feet hadn't moved this fast in weeks. I practically sprinted to Beth's minivan sitting in the parking lot. Thank goodness she was on time for once. She was sitting in the driver's seat, reading one of her romance novels, completely immersed in another world. I released the door handle, leaped in the passenger seat, and yelled at her, "Go, go, go!"

"Wow, it was that good, huh?" Beth smiled as she delicately put her book behind her seat.

"Great, wonderful, exciting. Now can we go?"

"Yes," she said as she turned the keys in the ignition. "Ice cream or home?"

"Home."

"Someone wasn't a good girl as promised, I see."

"Just had enough excitement for one evening," I said.

"C'mon, let's go get some cookie dough ice cream and pig out on your couch."

"Whatever."

"I'll take that as an enthusiastic yes."

We were pretty silent until we got back to the house. The trees along the sidewalks swayed in the Santa Ana wind. This was a pretty quiet neighborhood, minus the lawn mowers and occasional kid riding their bike, waiting for Mom or Dad to come home and fix their tablet so they could go back inside and be *normal* again.

We fell into our ritual and walked directly to the kitchen. Beth quickly grabbed the spoons, I tore off a few paper towels, and we met on the living room couch. She handed me my spoon as I threw some paper towels on her lap.

"So, are you going to tell me what happened tonight?" Beth asked.

"Why are you so interested?"

"Because I'm your sister and I love you."

"It was super boring."

"Well, I don't think it's designed to be a dinner-and-dancing type of function."

"You know what I mean. Just a lot of people who are seriously way too optimistic to be alive."

"What's so bad about that?"

"How can they be so happy when their loved ones are dead? I will never be like that. Never."

"As the old saying goes, never say never." Beth smiled as she grabbed her paper towel to wipe off the cookie dough drooling down her lips. "Anyway, I doubt they are happy their loved ones are dead. They're done with the initial part of the grieving process, that's all. They still miss them and love them, but they realize they must go on, because no good will come from obsessing about their loss."

"Maybe they didn't love them as much as I loved Chris," I said in a low tone.

Beth raised her voice slightly. "That's an awful thing to say."

"Well, maybe they didn't. Chris was all I had."

"No, he wasn't. You have me, Mark, the kids, Mom, your friends..."

"Whatever."

"You should hear yourself right now."

"Maybe I actually could hear myself if you weren't here," I said harshly.

"Fine." Beth stood up, went into the kitchen, slammed the freezer door, washed her spoon in the sink, and grabbed her coat. "I'll call you tomorrow."

"Whatever." I rolled my eyes.

"Lock the door behind me, please."

"I will."

"Love you, hon."

"Love you too, sweetie," I said sarcastically.

Beth shut the door behind her and left.

We always tried to say I love you when we parted. It was habit. Not necessarily a hug or a kiss or even a pat on the back, but usually an "I love you." When we were fighting, one or both of us would usually add a sarcastic "sweetie," "darling," or "hon" to the end of the sentence. This was to let the other one know we were angry—not that we usually needed a clue as to when the other one was angry. Even though we were four years apart, we knew each other well. The slight change of tone in our voices, the look in our eyes, our body language—we knew it all.

I knew when she was having one of those intense days of morning sickness that wouldn't go away when she was pregnant. Beth would always say she was fine over the phone or when I saw her, but I could read her. I was sure she wanted to tell me she was feeling like crap, that she was scared and needed help. But Beth held strong, pulled through, and gave birth to two sweet boys. She was the strongest person I knew besides Chris. I guess that now made her number one on my strong list. Lucky her. Guess that was one way to move up on a list of people: just wait for everyone else to die, and whoever was still living won.

Chris would always say I was the strongest person he knew. I would laugh and reply with some smart-ass remark like "Guess you don't know too many people then." He didn't get it. I wasn't strong at all. He should have known this. Why the hell didn't he see how *not* strong I was? How much I really needed him? Goddamn him.

CHAPTER 2

The doorbell was ringing. I shot straight up from the couch, a little confused. I stood up, looked around, and realized I must have fallen asleep on the living room couch last night. The doorbell rang again. I looked down and realized that I was wearing the same clothes I'd had on yesterday. I reached for my hair and found it meshed into a knot on the top of my head. I curiously walked to the door and glanced through the glass. It was Emma, one of the HR assistants from work. I quickly released the knot in my hair and tried to comb through the weeds. I took a deep breath and hoped it didn't smell as bad as I suspected it did. I opened the door and attempted to smile.

Emma's eyes grew big in reaction to my appearance. "Kara, I'm so sorry. We are all so sorry." She stepped forward and gave a clumsy but friendly hug.

I smiled and thanked her. I hadn't been at work for what seemed like ages. I had used my allotted three days of bereavement leave and my sick time, and they were letting me work from home for the next few weeks. It seemed odd to me that bereavement leave was only three days. After three days, I couldn't even have left the house, let alone gone to work. I had spoken to Valerie, the firm administrator, a week after Chris's death. She actually made the offer for me to work from home for the next month or two. My job was primarily legal research and drafting documents for attorneys to review, all of which I could pretty much do from home anyway, but it was nice that they had offered.

"Well, I brought your stuff from your desk like you requested." Emma leaned down and picked up a box. "Where do you want it?"

"Oh, I can grab that," I said as I took the box from Emma and put it near the couch.

"Great. Can you come out to my car and help me with the rest?"

"The rest?"

"Oh, there's three more boxes out there. They mostly are notes and files I was told to bring over," Emma said.

"Sure." Shit, I hadn't realized how much stuff I was going to have to actually do. I needed to get myself together.

After we piled the last box in the living room, I offered Emma some iced tea. She accepted, and we made our way into the kitchen. Thank goodness Beth had come by and helped clean the house yesterday. Hell, let me be honest, she cleaned the house. Beth really was the best. I needed to remember to apologize to her later.

"So, how are you holdin' up?" Emma asked with a warm smile.

"Oh, day by day, I guess. How's everyone at the office?"

"Good. Good. Same old, same old, you know. Harrison is gearing up for trial, so everything is rush, rush, rush, and the new receptionist we hired seems to be working out."

"Good. I thought I spoke to someone else when I called in last week. What happened to Melony?"

"She ended up getting a job closer to home. You know she commuted from Victorville."

"Yeah, that's rough." I nodded.

An awkward silence followed, but Emma quickly added, "We all miss you and hope you'll stop by the office when you're up to it."

"Thanks, Emma."

"I'd better get back, but it was great seeing you."

I walked Emma to the front door. "Thanks again for bringing my stuff by."

"No problem."

"Please tell everyone hi for me, and I will try and start on those briefs that Serena emailed me this weekend."

"Sounds good. Take care." Emma reached out for another quick hug and ran out the door. I closed the door behind her, sank to the floor, and began weeping. I didn't know why or where it had come from, but I couldn't stop it. It had been really nice to see Emma but so hard at the same time. Chitchat just seemed so superficial now. I really just wanted to be left alone.

Unfortunately, I still needed to work because I needed a paycheck. I was lucky Chris had made decent money as a professor, and we had some stashed away from his published work, but I couldn't live off of that forever. I shouldn't have been here sitting on the ground bawling my eyes out. I should have been at work thinking about Chris, thinking about what he was going to make for dinner, or asking myself if we would have time to go for our evening walk together. Not any of this crap. Not now.

Just as I finally gathered the strength to stand up and make my way to the bedroom to take a nap, the house phone rang. I climbed into bed and heard my home answering machine kick on.

"Hi, Kara, this is Mike from the COPE meeting last night. I'm sorry we didn't have a chance to speak after the meeting, but I wanted to give you my cell number. It's 555-5545. Please feel free to call me anytime, and I look forward to seeing you at the next meeting. Maybe we can meet a few minutes before or after to talk. Or we can schedule a formal session if you would like. Take care and see you soon."

Dammit, how had he gotten my number? I let out a loud sigh. I bet Beth had contacted him. I rolled over in bed, closed my eyes, and hoped I would wake up from this nightmare soon. When I opened my eyes, the room was dark, so the sun must have set already. I lay in bed trying to figure out what time it was. I guessed five thirty. I glanced at the alarm clock and it read 8:37 p.m. The answering machine was beeping. I slowly got up, stretched my arms, and went to the bathroom to wash my face. I stared at the stranger in the mirror. I was like one of those horrible pictures you see of people before they have makeovers or plastic surgery. How had that happened? The eyes were the same, just more red than blue these days. I whispered to myself, "What are you doing?"

I pulled my shoulder-length, light-brown hair into a sloppy ponytail and headed downstairs. I was hungry but couldn't figure out what to eat. I opened the fridge and scanned the inside for what seemed like minutes. I finally grabbed the milk, discovering that apparently I had to drink the entire full carton tonight, because it was due to expire at midnight. I found a clean bowl and spoon in the rack next to the sink and reached for the Special K sitting on top of the fridge.

I remembered the many cereal dinners Chris and I had shared together and smiled to myself. We had teased that was one reason why we would have been horrible parents. We would have said, "Hey, kids, everyone grab your favorite box of cereal and meet in front of the TV." To this day, at thirty-seven years old and my mother at sixty, she would roll her eyes when I told her I ate cereal for dinner. As if cereal was worse than a sixteen-ounce steak, onion rings, and a milkshake to wash it down. Chris had done most of the cooking. He was much better at it than I. I never found it fun or relaxing or whatever else people called it. I found it to be the worst possible punishment ever. I would rather have folded laundry, ironed, or vacuumed all day if it got me out of making dinner.

Growing up, we rarely went out to eat. Mom would cook breakfast, lunch, and dinner unless she was deathly ill, and even then, she would make TV dinners and lay them out for us. That was my mom: super mom. She was amazing. Mom worked as a bookkeeper during the day and had still managed to have time to volunteer at least once a week at the food bank, belong to the PTA, sew badges on our Girl Scout uniforms, and have dinner on the table by 6:00 p.m. sharp. After Beth and I had finished clearing the table and doing the dishes, Mom was always eager and ready to help us with our homework. I wondered how she had done all of that with little to no sleep. Chris and I had teased her sometimes about being a robot. She was still the same woman, full of energy and life. Unfortunately, she had extremely painful arthritis through most of her body and had had a knee replacement two summers ago. Mom had stayed with Chris and me for eight weeks after the surgery. The twins were still pretty young then, so we didn't expect Beth to have to take care of Mom too. Chris had offered to help out, since he was off for the summer and could still write at home while taking care of Mom.

Chris and Mom always got along very well. They both loved reading the newspaper in the morning, drinking black coffee, and watching Clint Eastwood movies. They were cute when they did their Eastwood impressions. Mom and Chris were both pretty terrible but always made us laugh.

I remembered one time when Mom teased him about it, and Chris had smirked. "You don't know what you're talking about," he said. "I sound just like Clint Eastwood."

"What the hell are you talking about? You sound like Sean Connery with marbles in his mouth!" Mom had said as she passed me the bowl of mashed potatoes.

"That doesn't even make sense. Clint Eastwood isn't Scottish, is he?" Chris asked.

"I know. I have no idea what you're doing! I think you need to get your damn ears checked!" Mom yelled back. We all laughed.

I smiled as I remembered my mom and Chris laughing. Both of them had been hilarious together. They could make me laugh till I cried. Well, now I cried at the drop of a feather, but before...you know. As I got older, I really understood all that Mom had done for us growing up. Her life had been us, and she'd always made me feel safe.

My dad had worked hard and died young, so we hadn't seen him much. Oh, and his mistresses had kept him pretty busy too. How my mother put up with his lying and cheating I would never know. It was so embarrassing. Everyone knew, so it seemed, that my father was cheating on my mother, except my mother. I used to ask Beth how a woman who could make her own toothpaste not realize her husband was cheating on her. But as I grew older, I realized she wasn't dumb at all. She knew he was cheating but chose to live in denial. Then as we got even older, the subject came up every so often, and she would blame it on us: "Oh, well, we wanted to stay together for you and Beth."

"That's ridiculous. Why would it matter if you and Dad were divorced?" I would ask.

"It was the times, Kare. You don't understand what family values mean."

"Guess not, because if Chris cheated on me once, I would be out the door in an instant."

"Well, that's your prerogative, isn't it?" she would say in her sarcastic, mean-mom tone. Beth would usually butt in by this time and ask if we were hungry, or if we could help her fold the towels, or something stupid so we would stop irritating each other.

Now I wonder if I would really have left Chris if he had cheated on me. Would I have really had the guts to be alone, by choice? Chris and I had been together for so long, I forgot what it was like to be single. The thought of not having someone balance the checkbook, make me tea when I was sick, or yell at me when I was being selfish or stubborn made me shudder. The funny thing was, once in a while, before Chris died, I used to remember my single days and long for a night out with my friends without responsibilities. Before any of us got married, my friends and I would go to the beach, take long drives, or go to bars, all for the purpose of having fun and meeting hot single guys. That was another life ago. Another person's life. Now all I wanted was Chris. I would have loved to hear his horrible Clint Eastwood impersonation one more time, to feel his touch, his kiss, or to hear him laugh. I rolled over in bed, held his pillow in my arms, and closed my eyes.

CHAPTER 3

Chris and I met in college. We were both English majors and had seen each other in different classes from junior year on. He was tall, with sandy blonde hair, and dark brown eyes. He dressed like Johnny Cash and didn't smile much, but when he did, he lit up the room. He was charismatic, and something drew people to Chris. I thought he must be playing up the starving-student, tortured-artist thing. We were paired up in one of our classes for a project and had to present on Samuel Beckett's *Waiting for Godot.* Chris and I had endless conversations about religion, philosophy, and life. I found out Chris was a pessimistic realist. He had so much excitement and charm when he was talking about things that he found interesting. I found myself missing the words and just watching his facial expressions. He was extremely expressive, and I could watch him for hours. I know this makes me sound like a serial killer, but it was true. Usually my fade back into reality came when he asked, "Are you even listening?" I would nod and say, "Let's move on." After we started dating, toward the end of junior year, he told me he thought he was boring me and that was why I would zone out. I agreed that he'd caught me and that was totally it. He knew I was not telling the truth and kissed me anyway.

We both graduated at the same time. I was excited for graduation, but nervous about where our lives would be taking us after we earned our degrees. Chris was brilliant and could do anything. He was accepted to multiple graduate schools throughout the country. I remembered the night of graduation, after the parties and well wishes assuring everyone we would all stay in touch, it was just me and Chris. We sat on my front porch. Everyone had gone to bed hours ago, and the street was silent. It was pretty dark on the block except for the few porch lights and streetlights. Chris took my hand gently in his and looked into my eyes.

"I love you," he said quietly.

This wasn't the first time Chris had told me he loved me; he just seemed serious this time, like an adult.

I started to giggle.

"You're drunk," I said as I tossed my bangs out of my face.

"What? No. I love you. I want you to know that," he said seriously.

I tried to collect myself, but I was a little drunk, and the giggling was hard to control.

"I love you too."

We kissed softly. It felt like minutes but must have

been much longer, because when I drew a breath, I realized the sun was beginning to rise.

Chris was smiling. He pulled out a ring box from his jacket pocket and got down on one knee.

"Kare, I love you. I want to be with you forever. I'm going to grad school in Washington and want you to come with me. Let's get married!"

I was shocked. Well, maybe shocked is the wrong word. Perhaps surprised sounds better. I'd had a feeling Chris was going to go to graduate school in Washington, but I didn't think he would ask me to go with him. I had been so worried about him breaking up with me, or us trying to balance a long-distance relationship. I truly wasn't expecting a marriage proposal. I hadn't planned on going to graduate school myself. I wanted to continue to work at the law firm where I was currently employed. I had started working there as a part-time receptionist during my freshman year in college and really enjoyed it. They liked me too and had promoted me to legal secretary about a year earlier. The plan was I could work full time now that I'd graduated from college, and then eventually get my paralegal certificate. I had not planned on leaving Southern California to do so.

By the look of bewilderment on his face, Chris must have sensed my hesitation. "I know, it's a lot to ask. To get married and move away. But I don't want to lose you. Graduate school will be done in about two years, and we can always come back."

I just sat there. My mind was racing but not making

any sense. The buzz had worn off, and I felt like I wanted another drink.

"Yes, I love you too. I want to be with you. I want to marry you!" I yelled.

He put the ring on my finger, and we kissed a long and passionate kiss. We then just held each other. It felt good. I felt safe and loved. I dug my face into his chest. I realized I would never want to forget this moment, so I smelled Chris and grabbed him tighter. His cologne still lingered on his clothes, and so did the alcohol on his lips.

Between getting ready to move, and planning a wedding, the summer went by quickly. Chris and I opted for a ceremony at the courthouse and then a small reception in my mother's backyard. It was perfect. The wedding was simple and elegant and just us.

My mom, Beth, and my best friend, Dawn, stood next to me during the ceremony, and Chris had his parents and his brother next to him. Chris had an estranged relationship with his parents. He grew up in a nice neighborhood in Pasadena with every material thing you could have ever wanted. His dad was a cardiologist, and his mom was a pharmacist. Chris said he didn't see his parents much growing up. They were always working, at some charity banquet, or taking a long weekend vacation away from work and their two sons. John was two years younger than Chris, although sometimes he seemed older. He was the typical athlete, captain of the football team, fun guy to be around. He was much more outgoing than Chris. He was also very handsome like

Chris, but in a different way. Chris had that hot professor thing going on, and John had the hot jock thing down. In grad school Chris got tired of wearing contacts all of the time, so he wore his glasses more often, which added to the sexy nerd look. John and Chris looked similar, with a tall physique, but John took after his father and had blue eyes, dark hair, and more of a square chin.

Despite Chris being a nerd, as we all lovingly teased, and John being into sports, Chris and John had a very close relationship. Probably because they'd leaned on each other a lot during their childhood. Chris said they looked out for one another. When their dad, Martin, was in a mood and had been drinking, they would warn each other and watch after their mother, Janet. His dad would like to throw things if he'd had too much to drink. Chris admitted to me that his dad had used his belt more than once on him and John. He saw his dad push his mom one time but never strike her. Their mother was also a drinker, but she was more of just a yeller. About once or twice a year, when Janet found out Martin was cheating again, she would throw his suits in the pool, and he would stay at a "friend's house" for a few days while she cooled off. Despite everything, their parents were still married, and pulled off happy appearances pretty well for the most part. But there was a lot of pent-up anger in that family. Martin was livid when Chris told him he was not interested in following in his or John's footsteps of becoming a doctor. Martin couldn't understand why someone would want to throw their life away studying literature. There wasn't a ton of money in it, and, according to Martin, it wasn't a real career. Janet was a little more understanding; however, it didn't do much good. Martin was about a foot taller and could be much louder than she was. He was definitely the head of the household and never let anyone forget it. Chris said his dad loved to argue and debate. Ironically, Chris had this feature as well, and it was one of the things that made him such a great writer, to Martin's chagrin.

My family was extremely different. When we were mad at each other, you knew it, but then we were over it pretty quickly. Chris would argue there was no point in fighting and preferred the passive-aggressive approach he had become accustomed to, probably because he was exhausted from fighting with his dad. I told him it was a release for us. It actually felt good to yell at my sister when she was being too bossy, or my mom when she was being too opinionated. It was okay that they yelled at me when I was being a brat and needed to come back to reality.

Chris's parents were not thrilled with Chris and me getting married. First, I thought maybe it was because we were young, and they didn't want Chris to be tied down. Or that I wasn't good enough for their son. Chris said his parents would never be happy with whomever he married and not to worry about it.

I found out early on in our relationship that Chris didn't want any money from his parents. Chris said his dad was pissed when he told him at the end of freshman year that he'd decided to declare English as his major. Martin told Chris he would no longer pay for an education that would get him nowhere, that it would be a waste of money. Chris agreed his father should no longer pay, and they didn't speak much after that except for the mandated birthdays and holidays. Chris continued to work at the campus bookstore and got a second job at the coffeehouse near campus. He used as much money as he could spare to pay for school and took out student loans to pay the rest. Chris vowed never to take any money from his parents, even when they offered to pay for a lavish wedding or graduate school. Chris said he didn't want his father to have the satisfaction of helping him or be able to take credit for any of the success in his life.

CHAPTER 4

The days all ran together. It was now the weekend, and I had told Emma I would begin working on those briefs. I pulled everything out of the boxes and set up on the dining room table. I was just going to go upstairs to take a little nap from all of this thinking when I heard the back door. It was Beth.

"Hey, what's going on?" Beth asked. Mark was right behind her with Ben and Elijah.

"Hi, you guys." I stood up and gave them each a hug and a kiss. It felt good to see the twins. They could always put a smile on my face. After a few minutes of talking, Mark took the boys into the living room. I was sure Beth had told Mark to do this before getting here. She was a planner. Beth had wanted to put me in a good mood, so she'd brought the kids, and then she would corner me alone in the kitchen. I knew her too well.

"So, what's been going on? It's good to see you up and about. Is this all work stuff?" Beth asked, trying not to raise too many questions all at once. I know it was eating her up inside.

"Yeah, Emma brought by my desk stuff. I was going through the boxes and getting everything organized."

"That's great. Do you need any help?" Beth's eyes sparkled.

"No, I'm good. Thanks."

"I'm sorry about the other day. I didn't mean to push you so much," Beth said softly.

"I know. I'm sorry. You do so much for me, and I really do appreciate it. Even if I don't act like it."

We hugged it out.

"Did Dr. Mike call you?"

"Dr. Mike? You mean the therapist guy?" I asked facetiously.

"Yes."

"Hmmm, I don't know. Maybe. I haven't checked all of my messages."

"Okay. So, he called, and you didn't call him back?"

"Maybe."

"Ugh. You drive me crazy." Beth rolled her eyes. "Please just talk to him. He is a great guy and can really help."

"He's like twenty years old. What does he know? Besides, I'm fine. I will be fine. You worry too much." I felt my voice raising.

"Well, he knows more than you think. He is actually forty-something, highly regarded, and has experienced loss in his own life. His mother died at a very young age, which is why he went into his field to begin with."

"Oh, okay. Good for him," I said.

After going back and forth like this with Beth for about another thirty minutes, including yelling, tears, and more hugs, I agreed to call Mike.

I dialed Mike's number and reached his voicemail. I left a message saying, "This is Kara. I will arrive at the next meeting a few minutes early so we can speak." It felt like my voice got higher with every word that came out of my mouth. I had tried to sound upbeat and hoped it didn't come out sounding crazy.

I surprised Beth when she came by the house to get me ready for the second meeting. I was awake and had taken a shower earlier in the day. She helped me comb my hair and we chatted about the twins. I was having an okay day. I needed to be better for Beth and for the twins. I would try.

Beth dropped me off at 6:00 p.m., and I caught Mike's side glance as I walked into the classroom. A bunch of people were already in the room, standing around and chatting. Mike made his way toward me and greeted me with a big smile. I followed him next door into an empty classroom.

"Thanks for coming. I'm glad we have some time to get to know each other."

"Sure," I tried to say enthusiastically.

"Okay, I'll start. Well, my name is Mike, and I have been working in the COPE group for about seven years now. My mother committed suicide when I was nine years old. I blamed myself for a very long time; then I blamed my dad for an even longer time. It took me years of therapy and self-realization until I understood it was neither one of our faults. She was ill. It was her decision to leave us. Unfortunately, we did our best to help her, and it just was not enough for her."

Silence ensued for a few moments and then Mike continued.

"That's the thing with losing someone. It's hard on us when someone dies. We miss them, we long for them, and we question why they are gone. We do the same in suicide deaths, which also include feelings of shock, blame, shame, guilt, and anger. We all deal with death differently. It's a process. There's no cure for it, but as you begin to heal, some days will feel better than others. Sometimes good days turn into good weeks and months, but know that experiencing grief is normal, and there is no specific time limit as to when you should feel better. Every situation and every person is different."

"Okay, I see," I said quietly.

"Well, since I poured my heart out, do you want to tell me a little about yourself? About Chris?" Mike asked.

It took me a minute to find the words I wanted to say. No one had asked me to tell them about Chris in a very long time. Chris was Chris. Everyone knew him. Everyone loved him. I felt myself losing it and began to cry.

"I'm sorry. This is so embarrassing," I stuttered.

"Never apologize for your feelings." Mike grabbed a handkerchief from his jacket pocket and handed it to me. I dabbed my eyes.

"Thank you."

Mike looked at his watch. "Well, time's up. Just kidding. If you feel like staying after and talking, let's do it tonight. If not, call me anytime, or come early again next time so we can continue our conversation. I'm persistent."

"You sound like my sister, Beth."

"Yes, I can tell you both share a very special bond."

"Definitely."

I handed Mike his handkerchief and stopped at the bathroom before going into the meeting. I washed my face with cold water and stared at myself in the mirror. I heard a toilet flush, and Mary popped out from one of the stalls.

"Hey there—Kara, right?"

"Yes. Mary, right?"

"Good memory. I remember it took me weeks to figure out who was who here."

I cracked a smile.

"Glad to see you back," Mary said as she washed her hands.

"Thanks. I would say it's good to be here, but you know."

"I know. It's not. None of us should be here," Mary said solemnly as she walked out the door with her head down.

I entered the meeting and took a seat between Jan and Mary. I learned during the meeting that Mary's son, Travis, had committed suicide a week before his high school graduation. I had assumed he was still alive, because at the last meeting she'd said she wanted to see her son graduate high school. It had never occurred to me he was dead, and she would never fulfill her wish. She still struggled with why he took a gun, put it in his mouth, and pulled the trigger. She shared the story of what happened. Mary had come home from work and started dinner that Wednesday evening. She hadn't expected Travis to be home for another hour because he had basketball practice. Mary had gone into the garage to start a load of laundry in between cooking dinner and making lunches for tomorrow. She had gotten pregnant at seventeen, and the father opted to go to college rather than stick around and help out. His parents had sent him to the East Coast and she never heard from him again. Her mom and dad had helped raise Travis. He was a great kid. He loved to read, ride his bike, and play basketball. She never realized how much pressure he had put on himself to do well in school and to play basketball. His suicide note explained he couldn't take the pressure of trying to do it all, and he said he was sorry. Mary later found out Travis was a closet alcoholic. She had no idea. It explained his mood swings and tiredness, but she'd thought that was all related to being a teenager. She blamed herself for not noticing the signs. She blamed herself for not really knowing her son.

Mike and the group were very supportive and listened to her, telling her she was not alone, and her son had his demons, as we all do, and it was no one's fault. My heart broke for Mary and Travis. I realized I was feeling sympathy for Mary and had forgotten about

Chris for a few moments. I felt guilty for not thinking of Chris; however, I couldn't imagine losing a child. I had never had any children, but just the thought of one of my nephews or niece not being here anymore crushed my heart. It would be unbearable.

After the meeting, as people were putting away tables and chairs, and gathering coats and purses, Elliot walked by and asked if I wanted to get some coffee with him and the others. I thanked him for the offer and told him my sister was waiting for me. But it made me feel good he had asked. Was that a good thing? Should I want to be in this group? No, of course not. Like Mary said, none of us should be there.

CHAPTER 5

I should have noticed the symptoms of depression. It should have dawned on me that what Chris was experiencing was not normal. Chris was always a sweet and interesting guy to be around. He loved a great conversation and made everyone feel important. I loved that about him. He had his off days or weeks, like all of us, so I didn't think much about it when he was moody, didn't want to talk, and kept to himself for days at a time. He was a writer. Writers are eccentric and weird sometimes, so I chalked it up to that. And stress. He was under a lot of stress in grad school. He had always pushed himself to go above and beyond with everything he attempted. Especially once he decided to continue on to get his PhD. We were young, living off of student loans and my job as a legal assistant at a small law firm, which didn't pay much. Chris worked on campus and did tutoring on the side as much as he could.

I remembered it was a Wednesday, and I had gotten home from work a little later than usual because my boss had told me she was pregnant, and we were chatting away after quitting time. I walked into our tiny one-bedroom apartment and noticed that the bathroom door was open and the light was on. I looked inside and it was empty. I heard sobbing. It took me a minute to realize it was coming from the bedroom. I stood at the doorway very quietly and heard Chris. The room was completely dark, but I could still see our full-size bed, which managed to take up the entire room. Chris was under the covers, and I couldn't see anything except for the top of his head. I ran into the room, turned on the light, and sat on the bed next to him.

"C, what's wrong? Are you sick? Do you need anything?"

"No," he said gruffly.

"What's wrong?"

"I don't feel good. Can you shut off that damn light?"

"Sure," I said as I ran to shut the light off as fast as I could. "Did you cancel your tutoring session?"

"What? Can you just leave me alone?"

"C, you're scaring me. What's going on? What can I do for you?" I was trying to hold back my tears of frustration.

"Just leave me alone. I don't feel well. I'll be better later. Please leave me alone right now."

"Okay. I love you." I tried to softly kiss the top of his head, but he shuddered away from me.

Chris stayed in bed for seven days like that. He only got up to use the restroom. He didn't even eat or drink anything that I ever saw. I left plates of food and water in the room, but I never saw him get up. I slept on the couch, and I called and emailed his professors and clients, explaining he was very ill and apologizing for his absence. I tried to continue on with my life as if everything were fine. Chris was just sick. He had a horrible migraine or something. He would be great in a few days or so. I would come home from work, and he would be there with dinner ready, and an apology for acting so abrasive. He would explain he'd just felt awful and not himself. Chris would say he loved me and promise it would never happen again.

The following Wednesday night, I arrived home and could immediately tell Chris wasn't there. His house keys and bus pass were not on the counter, and dishes were in the sink. At least he'd finally eaten something. I texted him to see if he was okay. He responded he was on his way home from work and would pick up Chinese food for dinner. I was thrilled.

I tore all of the sheets from the bed and threw them in the stackable washer. It was convenient having the stackable washer and dryer in the apartment. There was a small laundry closet next to the bathroom. The only problem was when you did laundry, there was nowhere to get away from the sound. I wouldn't have been surprised if all of the neighbors could hear that damn thing. No one ever complained, though, and I never heard anyone else's washer or dryer going, so I guess we were lucky to have thick walls.

Chris had left the jeans, sweater, and boxers he had worn for the past week on the floor, near his makeshift night table, which was made out of a stack of books. I looked through all of his pockets to see if I could find a clue as to what had been going on with him. Nothing.

Chris got home about forty-five minutes later with the delicious-smelling Chinese food from the restaurant across street that we both loved. He walked in with a smile on his face, kissed me on the cheek, and placed the food on our coffee table aka the dining room table.

"How was your day?" Chris asked as he started opening the plastic food cartons.

"Good. I got all of the month-end billing stuff done, so my boss was happy."

"Awesome," Chris said while trying to chew and keep his mouth closed.

"So, what's up with you?" I asked as I started hunting for the egg rolls.

"All good. I caught up with Professor Watson about my research paper, and he was pretty on board with the topic I chose and the direction I'm going."

"Very cool. I knew he would be. You're the best."

"I know." He chuckled and gave me a swift kiss on the cheek again. I sat down next to him on the couch.

Chris grabbed the remote, turned on the TV, and began flipping channels.

"Um, so, are we going to talk about it?" I asked, trying to hold back the irritation in my voice.

"Talk about what?" he asked innocently, half listening while he stared at the television set.

I hit the mute button on the remote. He turned toward me, and his demeanor completely changed. His eyes looked red, like he had been crying, and his smile was completely gone.

"What the hell?" he said. "I just want to eat dinner and relax for a few minutes before having to start on this damn research paper, and you want to talk and grill me with questions. You need to relax."

"You were in bed for a week and wouldn't talk to me, and now you're awake and acting like nothing happened. What the fuck is wrong with you? You can't do that. You need to tell me what is going on. I'm your wife! I'm here for you. I don't understand." I could feel my face getting warm.

Chris's tone turned softer. "I don't know. I was just having a bad day. I felt super tired, stressed, and worn out. I just needed a little break from everything. I needed to gather my thoughts and get focused."

"I totally understand that, C, but you were in bed for seven days. That isn't normal. We all have bad days and want to curl up and hide from the world, but we can't. Is there something else going on?" I asked sincerely.

"No, what? What do you mean?" He started getting defensive.

"I heard you crying sometimes."

We were silent for a few moments. I regretted saying it out loud.

"I don't know. I was just feeling down. Whatever. It's not a big deal. I told you, I was just tired and stressed. I needed a little break. I feel better now. End of story."

"C, please, maybe we should go see someone. Maybe talk to your doctor, or try a therapist?"

Chris stood up from the couch, grabbed his coat, and started walking out the door.

"Where are you going?" I yelled.

"To get some fresh air," Chris said as he slammed the door behind him.

I finished washing and drying the sheets and comforter. I put the bed back together, took a shower, dried my hair, and went to bed. Chris still wasn't home. This was the biggest fight we had ever had. The biggest fight before this one was when I was having second thoughts about moving to Washington, but we had pulled through.

Chris eventually opened up and told me he'd had episodes like this when he was very young. His parents had sought help, and he was given several different types of medications to combat what the doctors thought might be early symptoms of bipolar disorder. Chris said he was told it was hard to diagnose in adolescents, but with his symptoms, the specialists felt the diagnosis was probable. He'd stopped taking the medication on his own during his senior year of high school. Chris said he felt better and was tired of the side effects from the pills. He said the drowsiness and nausea were constant, and he needed a break from all of it. Also, he was not supposed to drink alcohol while on the medicine, and he'd found out the hard way that it could make you extremely ill if you ignored the warning label. Chris said he had not had an episode like the recent one in many years. I encouraged him to go to the doctor, a therapist, anyone. He promised he would if it happened again.

Things seemed to be back to normal. Chris was working and going to school, and I was working. Our routines were back in full swing, and life was good again, although sometimes on my way home from work, I would think back to that night I had come home and found Chris in bed. I was afraid it might happen again. Unfortunately, I was wrong. It was actually going to get much worse.

CHAPTER 6

I loved Sundays. It was our time. Chris and I would spend countless hours on the hammock in our backyard just talking, laughing, flirting, kissing, and loving each other.

I remembered I loved digging my chin into his chest. I felt so close to him and comfortable in his arms.

"Hey, did you ever call Beth back?" Chris asked as he looked down at me.

"Call her back—she called? When?" I asked, staring up at him.

"Friday night, I think it was."

"Friday, and you're just telling me now?"

"I wasn't telling. I was asking if you called her back."

"How could I call her back if you never told me she called?"

"What do you mean? I'm sure I told you."

"Sure, like the last time."

"You talk to Beth pretty much every day. How important could it be?" He rolled his eyes.

"I don't know. She's only my sister, that's all."

"You should just live together and save on the phone bills."

"I'm sorry, just because I'm close to someone, it doesn't really affect your life, does it?" I asked rhetorically, but he answered. "Yes, it does affect my life when it takes your time away from me."

"Away from you? Away from you? How is that possible when all of your free time is spent on the computer, on the couch, or in bed?"

Chris got up and went inside. I lay on the hammock, staring at the sky. The last few Sundays had been like this. I was starting to hate Sundays.

Our fourteen-year anniversary was coming up in a few weeks. Chris had taken the summer off to focus on some personal writing. Neither one of us had said anything about our anniversary. Normally we planned it for months ahead of time. We didn't buy extravagant gifts for each other; instead, because we liked to travel, we made it a point to go on an anniversary vacation. Whether it was a long weekend or a week-long adventure, it was our special way of celebrating us.

About a week before our anniversary, Chris and I had met after work for dinner at our favorite Thai place. We talked about our day, and then out of the blue Chris asked, "Do you mind if we skip our anniversary this year?"

This had caught me completely off guard. I was looking forward to planning a trip. I was hoping we would reconnect while we were away.

"Um, sure. I guess."

"It's not that I do not want to go somewhere. I think I need to get some help. I think I need to check myself into a place. I love you, and I know I'm driving you away. I'm driving myself nuts and pushing you away at the same time. I don't want to lose you. I want to get better." Chris was staring directly into my eyes.

"C, of course. Oh my God. I am here for you for whatever. I love you so much."

"I love you too," Chris said. He grabbed my hand and kissed it. "I've been talking to a therapist, and he recommended a place in Northern California. It would be for about four weeks. Just to refocus and rejuvenate myself."

"Sounds good, C." I was shocked he had been seeing a therapist again. Happy but shocked.

"Are you taking any medications right now?" I don't know why this question popped out of my mouth. As soon as I said it, I wanted to take it back. It just was not the right place or time. I didn't want to say anything to upset him.

"Yeah, I was on something, but it was giving me really bad headaches, so I recently switched to a new medication. So far, the side effects are less. You probably noticed I've been really moody, and I'm so sorry. It is part me, part the meds, and part stress, I guess. It's not you at all. I don't want you to think it's you."

My heart was feeling full. "I'm here for you, C. Just let me into your life. I can help. Whatever you need."

"Thanks, I appreciate it. And all that you put up with."

"I'm not perfect." I smirked.

"Well, that I cannot argue with." We laughed.

Chris was gone for most of July and the early part of August. The house was too quiet. It was weird not having him around. Even though he had been distant lately, at least I knew he was in the other room.

The program advocated that family communication be limited in order to help the residents adjust to their new temporary lifestyle, therapy, and surroundings. Chris and I spoke on the phone once a week. I looked forward to hearing his voice. He didn't talk much about the therapy. Chris talked more about how beautiful the area was, and how he wanted to take a vacation with me there someday. That made me very happy. Nothing much happened at home. I just talked about work, my nephews, and how I was helping plan my co-worker's surprise bridal shower.

The program was only supposed to be four weeks, but Chris called about three weeks in and told me he was extending his stay an additional two weeks. I understood. As long as he came back happy and healthy, that was all that mattered.

Finally, the weeks had gone by, and the day came when Chris was coming home. I met him at the airport. He looked different. Good different. He had a short beard, looked a little leaner, even taller somehow. We talked all the way home. I made tacos for dinner, and then we sat outside by the pool.

"It feels good to be home."

"It's so good to have you home. I missed you."

"I missed you too," Chris said as he gently touched my face and kissed me. We hadn't kissed in a very long time. Not a kiss like that. It felt amazing. I felt like we were kids again. That night we made love and just held each other. We were back.

CHAPTER 7

The day of the funeral was a complete blur. I remembered the feel of the itchy black dress I'd found in the back of my closet. I didn't even remember where it had come from. Well, Beth had actually found it for me while rummaging through my closet as I sat on the edge of the bed, staring off into oblivion. Beth snapped me out of it as she threw the dress on my lap.

"Here, Kare, just wear this. It will be fine."

I just sat there. I didn't know what to do. My body couldn't move. I knew I needed to get up and put this stupid dress on, but my legs stayed put. I don't know how long I sat on the bed. It must have been a while because Beth was already dressed and had her makeup on when she came back to the room, and she always took forever to get ready. Beth would wear makeup to the gym. I love her. I hope she never leaves me like Chris did. My heart couldn't take it.

I felt like a feather could have taken me out at this point. Beth jostled my clothes off and threw the dress on me like I was a rag doll. She combed my hair and wiped away my tears. When had I started crying? I didn't even realize I was shedding tears until she gently rubbed the tissues under my eyes. She knew better than to even try and attempt to put makeup on this face today. All of the makeup in the world would not help. I didn't care. This was what grieving looked like. This was what anger, shock, and disbelief looked like.

Beth guided me downstairs, where Mark and the twins were waiting. They all looked so handsome dressed up in their suits.

"Hey, Kara," Mark said softly as he wrapped his arms around me. "The car is here. You all ready?" He gently pulled away and started guiding the boys to the front door.

I didn't respond. No, I'm not ready, I thought. I'm not ready to say goodbye to Chris. It felt like he was going to walk in the door any minute. Like this was all a big practical joke, or he was at a boring conference and lost his cell phone so cannot contact anyone.

We all walked to the black limo Beth had rented. Why were we going in a limo? Why did people go in limos to funerals? Weren't they the designated cars for proms and weddings? How did funerals get lumped into the same category of events? I wondered if they saved a few black limos at the lot for all of the funerals. Was it acceptable to go to a funeral in a white limo? Did it matter? Nothing mattered. I should have rented a damn Porsche or something for this fucking day. It would have made the car ride more enjoyable. Actually, probably not.

We arrived at the church. Chris and I were not very religious, but his parents insisted on having a church service. I knew this was not what Chris would have wanted, but I didn't care. I didn't want him to like any of this. He didn't deserve the funeral he wanted. Chris and I had never spoken much about our plans for when we died. He was so against talking about death. He hated when I brought it up. I told him I would donate his body to science if he didn't care. Chris would always say, "So what, I'll be dead. What the hell do I care." Well, yeah, I guess you don't care. Obviously, you don't care because you are a selfish bastard who didn't care about anything. You played me a fool for so long. I wondered how long he had planned his death. Did he have second thoughts after he jumped? What did he think about right before he died? Did your life really flash before your eyes? Was he in pain, or was death instantaneous? I hoped it was quick. I wouldn't have wanted him to suffer. Even though, now, I was serving a life sentence of living like a dead person. I might as well have been on that ledge with him. I was angry he'd taken his life. I was also angry he'd taken my life with him.

A large photo of Chris at the front of the church startled me. I had forgotten what he looked like. He had just been this dark space in my head since that horrible day. His picture was staring at me down the church aisle. That smug son of a bitch. Wipe that goddamn smile off of your fucking face! I yelled at Chris in my head. Were you thinking of killing yourself when your brother took that photograph of you at the beach a couple of years ago?

I didn't realize I had been walking slowly up the aisle. I was suddenly face-to-face with Chris. He was smiling and looked so happy. His beautiful brown eyes were glowing, and his hair was magnificently tousled from the wind. I remembered that day like it was yesterday. John and family had come out from Santa Barbara to visit us on Memorial Day weekend, and we'd all gone to Corona del Mar for the day. It was a gorgeous, hot day. We all had such a good time swimming, boogie boarding, eating, laughing.

I noticed the urn next to the photo. John had helped me pick out the urn. It was simple and elegant. I couldn't believe that thing held what used to be a thirty-eight-year old, six-foot, hundred-and-eighty-pound guy. We couldn't have an open casket for obvious reasons. I didn't want to think about what Chris's body must have looked like after the fall. John had identified Chris at the morgue and I was sure it still haunted him.

John and his wife, Celine, were already seated in the front. Their kids, Noah, eight, and Isabella, five, were sitting in between them. Celine was whispering to the children, while John just stared at Chris's photo. I wondered if he was remembering that day at the beach too.

His parents, my mom, family, and friends all started arriving. We all gave each other long, forced hugs. I had not hugged this many people since my wedding day. I remembered how my jaw had hurt on our wedding night from all of the smiling and talking. Today my goal was not to say anything. I was sure other people felt the same way. What do you say to someone whose husband jumped off a sixteen-story building? "Sorry for your loss." "He is in a better place now." "He is no longer in any pain." I had heard it all.

After the minister finished the eulogy, John spoke for the family, and thanked everyone for coming. He told the story of when he and Chris went fishing and got lost hiking back. They'd spent the night out under the stars and woke up early the next morning to try and figure out where they were. After another hour of fumbling around, they realized they were less than a mile from the road where they had parked. Chris and John loved this story. I don't know exactly what happened that night, but Chris and John seemed to have each grown a deeper appreciation and love for one another after that time together, not to mention all of the inside jokes they shared.

In John's closing remarks, he invited everyone over to our friend Dawn's house after the service. After the funeral, more awkward hugs, and then silence followed. I found myself standing in front of Chris's photo again.

I suddenly felt someone grab my hand. I looked around and the room was completely empty except for my mom standing right beside me. Apparently, I hadn't realized the sanctuary had cleared out. I looked at Chris's picture one last time before my Mom led me out of the church, and we made our way to Dawn's house. Dawn was one of my closest friends. We had known each other since elementary school. When Chris and I moved to

Washington, Dawn and I spoke on the phone every day for a month. We missed each other very much. Dawn was such a caring and supportive person. She reminded me of Beth. Dawn got married a few years ago to Jason. He was a nice guy, beside the fact he was obsessed with golf, which was something we all teased him about. The four of us had tried to meet for dinner at least once a month. Jason also loved to cook, so he and Chris would often talk about recipes like two old ladies sitting on the porch on a Sunday afternoon.

Dawn had offered to host the post-funeral gathering at her house to give everyone a break. She knew Beth had been helping me out a lot and still had her own life to worry about. My mom would call me every day, but she wasn't as mobile as she used to be, and it wasn't easy for her to come over to the house as often. Dawn had lost both of her parents. Her dad died about ten years ago from cancer, and her mom suffered a massive stroke two years ago. She was an only child, and her parents' deaths had been hard on her. Dawn was so grateful her mom had walked her down the aisle at her wedding before she died. She felt bad her mom and dad would never see their grandbaby. Dawn was almost five months pregnant with a little girl. She planned on naming her after her mom, Matilda, Matty for short.

John and I found each other hiding out in Dawn's backyard. We didn't need to explain what we were doing out here. We both were avoiding the handshakes, hugs, tears, and memories that filled the house.

"How are you holding up, Kare?" John spoke so faintly, I almost thought it was Chris's voice.

"Surviving." Poor choice of words.

"Beth tells me you are having a hard time of it," John said somberly. "I'm sorry I haven't been calling much the past few days. You know, if you need anything, or I can do anything, call me anytime."

"I know. You don't need to worry about everyone, John. You need to take care of yourself too. I feel like an idiot. Beth takes care of me like I'm her third child, and I feel so embarrassed. I just don't care about anything anymore. This is what Chris must have felt like all of the time. Hating life and wanting everything just to be quiet. No wonder he wanted to escape it." I wiped tears from my eyes.

"Kare, he loved you. You gave him love, hope, purpose. He always said you were the best thing that ever happened to him, and we all know that is true. He was sick for a long time. Even before you met him. It was something internal. He would be fine for a while, and then all of a sudden he would shut down again, but he always came back up. Chris was a fighter. He was my hero." John looked away. I could tell he'd started crying too.

"That was a nice picture you picked out for the funeral. I love that photo of Chris. We had a great day that day," I said.

"Yes, we did. The best part was when Chris snorted soda up his nose." John smiled.

"Oh yeah, I remember that. Chris had made a joke

about your receding hairline, and you said something back like, 'Well, at least I don't look like Mom.' And Chris lost it. He had just taken a big swig of soda when you said that and was not expecting a quick comeback. He started laughing and the soda totally went up and out of his nose." I started laughing.

"What a dork." John started laughing too.

Chris's parents came outside. We hugged and said pleasantries. I could tell his mom had been crying. Her eyes were red, and her makeup was smeared. Martin had the same arrogance about him, but he seemed smaller somehow. Not so threatening.

"Thank you for everything. If you need anything, please let me know," I said.

"Thank you, Kara. Chris was a very sweet boy, and with so many gifts," his mom said as she clutched her handkerchief.

"Yes, Kara. If you need anything, let us know," Martin said in a deep voice as he looked away.

We hugged again, and they left.

"Wow, I have never seen my dad look so old before," John said in a surprised voice.

"Yeah, he looked different."

"He looked sad," John said. "Chris would have loved the irony that Dad actually did have feelings for him, but they didn't show up until after he died." I wasn't sure if he was talking to me or himself, so I didn't say anything in response.

The day dragged on, and we finally said our final goodbyes to family, friends, Chris's current and former students, colleagues, and neighbors. It was a nice way to remember Chris. He had been important to many people. I don't think Chris realized how many lives he had affected. Maybe if he had, he would still be here today. It had only been nine days since Chris's death, but already felt like an eternity.

CHAPTER 8

A couple of weeks after Chris's death, I had to go meet with our accountant, Jeff. Beth and Dawn had both offered to come with me, but I didn't want them to think they had to babysit me while I figured out my finances. Jeff worked in an office building not far from Chris's school.

"Hey, Kare. I'm so sorry."

"Thanks, Jeff." We hugged, and I sat across from him in his office.

Chris and Jeff had been friends since high school. Jeff was a stereotypical accountant: kind of nerdy, but sweet and funny. He had married his high school sweetheart, Annie, and they had four beautiful daughters. Chris and I had always teased poor Jeff that he was the odd man out, literally.

"Okay, how bad is it?" I asked, trying to lighten the heaviness.

"Not bad, not great." Jeff started shuffling papers

around on his desk. "Well, you know the life insurance policy doesn't cover, you know, deaths like Chris's."

"Ones where the person jumps off a building. Yeah, I get it," I said. I wasn't mad at Jeff, but I was starting to get angry at Chris again.

"You guys have your savings and 401(k)s. Chris's car was paid off, so maybe you could sell that."

Yikes, I'd totally forgotten Chris's car was still parked at Beth's house. Beth and Mark had gone to pick it up for me, and left it at their house, sparing me having to look at it right now. I couldn't imagine selling it.

"Your mortgage is a little steep for a single income now. You can make it work. You would just need to budget a little more and not filter as much into savings each month."

"Wow, I didn't even think about having to sell the house." I looked down at my hands sitting in my lap.

"You don't have to, Kare. It's just an option. It just depends on how tight you want to live. We can make out a plan for you."

"Sure."

"You can always get a roommate. Or ask Chris's parents to help pay off the house."

"No, no way. Chris wouldn't take anything from them when he was here, and I'm definitely not going to take anything from them when he's gone. It's bad enough they helped out with the funeral expenses."

"No, I get it. But Chris didn't really plan this out for you, did he? You have to take care of yourself now, Kare." I was shocked how blunt Jeff was being.

"I'm surprised to hear you say that."

"Kare, I loved Chris like a brother, but I can still be pissed at him right now."

"Yeah, I get it. I am too."

In a strange way, it felt comforting to talk to someone who was also angry at Chris right now. Sometimes I forget that it wasn't just me he ran away from. Chris left all of us with unanswered questions and broken hearts.

"Kare, I'm not saying this stuff to be an asshole. I'm just giving you a reality check and want you to be set for your future."

"Thanks, Jeff. I get it, and I appreciate it."

We talked some more about the pros and cons of the different options. I left there feeling like a truck had just run me over. I agreed I would think about selling the car and house.

I stopped at the grocery store to buy a few things. I roamed around the aisles, just picking up random items. Once I got to the alcohol aisle, I realized all I had in my cart was chips, limes, milk, coffee, and cereal. I rolled my eyes at myself. I looked up and down the alcohol aisle for a while. I finally decided on three different bottles of wine, a weird can of sangria, and a case of Corona beer.

While I was waiting in line, I caught the side glimpse of two women at the next register, staring at me. I looked over, and they instantly evaded their eyes. I didn't recognize them, but maybe they had known Chris. I felt them staring at me as I emptied the grocery cart and put my items onto the counter. I felt like everyone was staring at me and whispering. I had to get out of there. The cashier rung me up, and I pushed the cart quickly out to my car. I swear I heard the two women laughing as I exited the store. I threw the bags in the trunk, pushed the cart to the side, and jumped in the car. I turned up my music really loud. "So Alive" by the Goo Goo Dolls was playing. I love you, Goo Goo Dolls, I thought, but seriously?! I quickly shut the radio off and wiped angry tears from my eyes.

I arrived home and put the groceries on the counter. I opened the first bottle of wine and took a big swig. Who the fuck needed a glass? No one was here. I went outside to the patio and just sat there staring at the pool. After the last sip of the bottle, I threw it against the wall of the house. Only half the bottle shattered. I couldn't even do that right! I ran back inside to open a second bottle. Halfway through it, I went into Chris's office. I opened the curtains to let the sunlight in. His office faced the pool and had a sliding glass door to the patio. The air felt old and stale in the room so I opened the door. I started rummaging through his desk. I didn't know what I was looking for, but I wanted to see what else he might have been hiding. I opened each drawer and started thumbing through papers and throwing them everywhere. I found a bottle of Scotch in the bottom of his third drawer.

"There you are, you fucker." It was about half full. I opened the bottle and took a drink. Whew, that burned. I'd forgotten how Scotch felt in my throat. Maybe that was why Chris had loved it. Maybe the burning made him feel alive. Scotch was his dad's choice drink too. I'd never liked it much, but I hated to see good alcohol go to waste. I started pulling books from the shelves and then noticed his golf bag in the corner. I grabbed the five iron and started swinging. After smashing the desk several times, I moved onto the bookcase. I destroyed the picture frames on the walls and gave the couch a few strong swings too. Then I grabbed a bunch of crap off the desk, went to the backyard, and threw it all in the pool. I went back for the golf bag and clubs and chucked them in too. I made several trips back and forth, just taking shit from his office, and throwing it into the pool. Afterwards, I just stood there watching all of Chris's meaningless possessions float aimlessly in the water. I took my shoes off and dove in headfirst. When I opened my eyes underwater, I saw Chris's belongings quietly dancing all around me. Taunting me. Panic quickly overran my thoughts, so I started to swim in order to escape. The water was freezing, and my body felt limp, but I continued to make my way to the deep end of the pool, shoving Chris's things out of the way as I pushed toward my final destination. I wondered how long I could hold my breath underwater. I continued to swim despite the lightheadedness closing in. I was losing my breath but fighting the urge to come up for air. The water and the darkness comforted me. I didn't want to return to the world. I wanted to stay at the bottom of the pool forever.

Eventually my reflexes kicked in, and I involuntary complied. I rose my head above the water to draw breath. The sun was almost gone, and the pool light had kicked on. It had taken my last bit of strength to get out of the pool. I grabbed the bottle of Scotch I'd left in Chris's office and went back outside. I lay on the deck chair and must have passed out because the next thing I knew, Dawn was shaking me awake.

"Kare, Kare, wake up!"

"I'm up," I said. It was dark outside. "What time is it?"

"It's eight thirty. What the hell happened here?!" Dawn motioned toward the pool and then Chris's office. The sliding door was still open, the curtains blowing in the wind. It probably looked like a tornado had gone through the room.

"I—I don't know." It was hard for me to completely open my eyes. I was so tired.

"Kare, are you okay?" She sat down next to me and moved the bottle of Scotch away.

"Yeah, yeah, just…you know."

"I don't even want to ask how it went today with Jeff."

"Don't. And that's not all of it."

"Come inside," she said as she rose and then helped me up. Poor Dawn, six months pregnant and having to help her stupid-ass friend out of a chair.

We went inside and she gently pushed me into one of the kitchen chairs.

"Let me make you some coffee."

"I don't want coffee. I just want to go to bed."

"In your condition, if you go to bed, you might not wake up."

"And the problem is?" I started to laugh inappropriately.

"Kare, don't do this. This isn't you. Come on. Tomorrow is a new day. We will get through this together."

I thought of all of the conversations I'd had with Chris saying the same crap over and over. Absolutely pointless. What a waste of time. No wonder Chris hadn't listened. If I'd sounded like Dawn, I wouldn't have listened either. What a nag I had been.

Dawn looked at the groceries lying on the counter.

"What is this? Are you a goddamn child? You need to eat something."

She opened the fridge and found a bunch of meals Beth had prepped for me in different-sized Tupperware containers with easy-to-read labels. I was pathetic. Dawn grabbed one of the containers and put it in the microwave. Within the next ten minutes, I had a glass of water, coffee, and a container full of chicken and rice in my face. I felt like I was going to be sick, but Dawn said she wouldn't leave until I'd had some. I ate a few bites and drank some coffee and water to make her leave.

Dawn helped me up the stairs to bed.

"Please don't tell Beth," I begged. "She doesn't need to worry about me. She already does too much."

"We'll see."

Dawn made me change out of my wet clothes before I climbed into bed. She tucked me in and shut off the light. I could still hear her downstairs cleaning. She should have gone home to Jason.

I faded away pretty fast. When I woke up, it was still dark outside. I had to go pee so bad. I quickly ran to the bathroom and then back to bed. I lay there listening and didn't hear anything downstairs. I looked at the clock and it read 7:17 p.m. Holy shit, I'd slept an entire day again! I'd done that several times in the last couple of weeks. I rubbed my eyes and got out of bed. When I went downstairs, I saw Dawn, Jason, and Beth outside on the patio. I walked slowly outside. I felt like a teenager who was getting ready to face her parents after breaking curfew.

"Hey, sleepyhead. I was getting ready to go throw some cold water on you." Beth came over and gave me a warm hug.

"Hey, Kare. Ready to go dancing?" Jason teased and gave me a hug.

"Sure, let me get my shoes on, and we can go."

"Hey, sweetie." Dawn came over and also gave me a hug.

I noticed the pool had been cleaned and the broken wine bottle picked up. The Scotch was nowhere in sight. The sliding glass door to Chris's office was closed, so I guessed they'd cleaned that mess too.

"Thanks for cleaning up. I made a pretty big mess last night. Sorry." I sat down and stared at the concrete.

"No problem. We are just worried about you," Beth said.

"I just had a bad day. I'm better today." I gave a quick overview of my visit to Jeff's office and the women at the grocery store.

"Screw those women, Kare. But every time you think someone might be talking about you or Chris, you can't act out like this," Beth said sternly.

"I know, yes."

"We think you should try a group therapy session with others who have lost loved ones suddenly," Dawn said.

"You mean with losers whose husbands committed suicide?" I asked in a mean tone.

"Kare, don't be like that," Beth scolded me.

"We called Dr. Sinclair," Jason said gently. "We got her number from the card Detective Jackson left. She recommended this group called COPE. They meet every other Thursday at 6:30 p.m."

"Pass," I said as I shook my head. "You guys, I just had a bad day, that's all. It will be fine. Chris has only been gone a few weeks. Am I supposed to forget him and move on already? Sorry, I can't get over it that fast. Sorry I'm such a burden." I felt like such a baby saying that, but I couldn't help myself.

"No, of course not. We think it may just help to talk with others who have gone through similar experiences," Beth said lovingly.

We went back and forth for a while. I told them I would think about it and then went back to bed. Their persistence ended up paying off, and I went to a meeting about two weeks later. Little did I know, I would end up meeting some wonderful friends that really did help me through the worst time of my life. If it hadn't been for them, and my family, I would still be hiding in the deep end of the pool.

CHAPTER 9

Chris had left three notes in separate envelopes on his desk in his office at work. One was for me, one for John, and one for his parents. Till this day I still don't know what the other notes said. I never asked John or his parents, and they never asked me about mine.

Dear Kare,
Wow, sounds so formal. I wasn't sure how to start this. I wasn't sure if I should even leave a note, but then I thought that would have been even worse. I am so sorry. This is all me. There is nothing anyone could have done or said to stop this. I have been struggling for a long time. I had moments where I thought I was getting "better" or even "cured," and then a few weeks or months later, the heaviness just came back. It's haunting, and I'm just so tired of fighting it. I love you now and always. If it wasn't for you, I probably would have done this a long time ago. You were the only true

light in my life, and you deserve so much better. Please forgive me.
Love always,
C

I'd read this note a million times, and it still broke my heart every time. Yet, I still didn't completely understand it. Chris obviously had been hurting for a long time and I failed him. It was almost as if he was dying right in front of me and I did nothing to save him. I carried on with my own miniscule problems and barricaded myself in a wall of ignorance. Maybe I didn't want to know how Chris was really feeling. Could it have been that the idea of having a perfect life and marriage together was all that I cared about? Chris was wrong about one thing for sure. I didn't deserve better. He had deserved better.

The subject of suicide notes came up in group one night. Some people had received notes, and others hadn't. Monique was one of the latter.

"I don't know why she didn't even leave a note. Maybe it was an accident, and she didn't mean for all of those pills to kill her that day. Maybe it was a cry for help gone wrong. If one of us had gotten home sooner, maybe we could have saved her. Called the paramedics sooner.

"She looked so small on the floor. Her eyes half open, her body curled up into a ball. Vomit all over the rug. So much vomit. My baby sister choked on her own vomit. She was only twenty-two years old. What in the hell is the matter with this world? Her death almost killed my parents. Hell, it has, in many ways. We all blame ourselves. Nobody ever speaks her name at my parents' house. It's always the big elephant in the room. Pictures of Clarissa are all over their house. Clarissa staring at us. Smiling at us. Laughing at us. Yet, we don't even speak her name." Monique stared off into the distance. That must be what I looked like to Beth when I was off in my other dimension thinking about Chris.

There was silence for a few moments.

"My wife did the whole pills thing too," Frank said. "She lit candles all over our bedroom. How sick is that? She wanted to make it peaceful for herself, I guess. Goddamn room full of scented candles, and all you could smell was the fucking vomit. I still smell it. I can't even sleep in that room anymore. The smell is always there.

"She did leave a note. All it said was, 'Please forgive me. I can't do this again. I'm in heaven now. Love, Kelly.' Thanks for the note. Thanks for making me find your lifeless body in our bed. How can you do that to someone you love?"

Mike looked around the room. "I know we get on this topic every once in a while, and it can be very difficult. We have to remember that our loved ones were not thinking rationally. They felt alone, scared, and hopeless. That is no one's fault. Unfortunately, it just happens, and I know it may feel like they did this without thinking of you, or your feelings, but they did love you. The mind is just so incredibly powerful; it doesn't always let the love and compassion into the world they are living in."

"No, she wasn't thinking of anyone but herself," Frank said angrily. "She was not thinking of me, our three sons, or our grandchild when she did this. She could have beat the cancer again. I know she could have."

"My husband left me and my three children," Georgia said quietly. "I was very angry for a long time. I still get angry sometimes. I still don't know why he did it but have come to the realization it was his problem. Nothing we did caused it. Nothing we didn't do caused it."

"Well, at least you didn't find the body. He had the decency to shoot himself in the woods," Frank said quickly.

"At least you got a note. All I got was a 'love you all' on the back of an old receipt found in his pocket."

"Okay, okay," Mike chimed in. "We are not here to play the who-has-it-worse game again. There are definitely no winners, and we are all losers that play."

"My mom left me a long note," Layla said. "Three pages. It didn't make it any better that she did that. It still didn't bring her back to life."

"Good point," Mike said. "Receiving a note or not doesn't change anything. I think people may find comfort with a note or some sort of closure. But not always. Family and friends are often still left asking why."

A short silence followed again.

"My brother left a note in his jacket pocket," Elliot said. "He left it for his ex-girlfriend, Gina. She is the reason Jesse killed himself. She killed him. He loved her too much. I told him to take it slow and not rush into anything. She left him after six months. He stalked her, pleaded with her, threatening to kill himself if she wouldn't give him another chance. I tried talking to him. He was so unreasonable. All he talked about was Gina. Jesse was obsessed. He finally blew it one night, went over to her house, shot Gina, and then shot himself in her front yard. Gina was hit in the arm and the stomach and fortunately survived. Jesse died instantly. I had told him there would be other girls, but he just couldn't get over it.

"A few months after the incident, Gina let me read the note. It was ten pages of Jesse professing his love for her. One paragraph would be about how much he loved her; the next paragraph said he wouldn't allow her to be with anyone else. It was awful." Elliot got up and stared out the window. Jan walked over and started whispering to him. Mike joined them and spoke to them for a few minutes.

"My best friend drove his car off a cliff," Efrain said. "It's been three years, and I still can't believe he's gone. Alex was a complex person. He had mood swings. Some days he wanted to skip school and drive to Vegas for the day, and other days he could barely speak. He was seventeen. We were talking about graduation, what colleges we wanted to apply to. Then one night he sneaks out, takes his dad's Volvo, and never comes back. He was found the next morning by some hikers. I still don't know if Alex drove his car off the cliff on purpose, or if he was just pushing the limits that night and accidentally went too far. The police said there were no skid marks to indicate he wanted to stop, but he didn't leave a note, so we will never know the truth. The not knowing is what kills me. Kills his parents too." Efrain wiped his eyes.

Elliot, Jan, and Mike had rejoined the group in the middle of Efrain's monologue.

"I keep the note Carlos left with me at all times," Jensen said. He pulled out his wallet, removed a folded piece of paper, and read it aloud. "I am sorry. I know you won't understand, but this is something I have to do. See you on the other side. I love you more than anything. Don't hate me. Love, Car." Jensen put the note back in his wallet. "I am thankful he wrote it, but he's right, I still don't understand why he did it. I have started the process of forgiving, I think. I'm not as angry as I used to be, which is a good thing. But I didn't understand. He had a very supporting and loving family, even after he came out. He wasn't kicked out at fifteen and told he was going to hell by his family like I was. I had to live on the streets for a year until one of my friends who had a cool mom said she didn't care that I lived on the couch.

"Carlos and I had such different lives, yet he was the one that killed himself. There were so many times when I thought about offing myself. Especially when I was alone and felt no one would even notice if I were gone. The funny thing is Carlos probably saved my life. We met while working at a fast-food restaurant. He was going to college and working two jobs. He encouraged me to go back and get my GED. We soon fell in love and got married. We were living the life. Had good jobs, a nice place, thinking about adopting. Yeah, his job was stressful sometimes. Maybe I didn't realize how stressful. He didn't like to talk about his work much. He said it would have bored me listening to stats and accounting jargon. You never know. Never take anything for granted." It almost seemed like Jensen was talking to himself. Ruben sweetly patted Jensen on the shoulder.

"It's the same story over and over again, right?" Ruben asked. "What should we have done? What could we have done? Why them and not us? It sucks. My sister, Jasmine, was seventeen when she slit her wrists. We were twins. I should have known. We knew so much about each other. She had first tried to kill herself by slitting her wrists when we were fifteen. That was a definite wake-up call. She had tests, followed by so many doctor and therapy appointments; she even went away for a while to a 'special clinic' to help 'heal.' She tried to kill herself a second time by attempting to hang herself with a sheet when she was at the special clinic. I guess it was only a matter of time before she finally got it right.

"She struggled in school, was a loner except for a few loser friends and boyfriends along the way. I tried to talk to her, but she shut me out. She shut out my parents, everyone. All of the medicines, therapy, and all that didn't do anything except piss her off even more. I hate saying this, and it took me a long time to admit out loud, but I felt a bit of relief when she died. What the fuck is wrong with me? How could I feel that way? I realized it was because she was the source of all our family's attention. I was the A student, star of the track team, on the school newspaper. None of that mattered. My parents took off so much work and personal time for Jasmine that they had no energy left for me or my activities, and it pissed me off. She acted horrible and got all of the love. I just disappeared into the background. I wish I could have done more. I wish I had been more understanding about it all. Not a selfish, stupid high school kid, worried about myself. It's eleven years later, and I still feel like an asshole. I hope Jasmine can forgive me." Ruben looked toward the ceiling.

Sal gently patted Ruben on the back.

"Most of you guys all know the story of my grandson, Jacob," Sal said. "He was a beacon in my life. His dad, my son Abraham, and I were very close. We would celebrate all holidays together, the Sabbath every week, and my wife and I would care for Jacob after school while Abraham and his wife, Rachel, worked. Jacob would follow me around the house, and I would show him everything from how to properly trim a rose bush to how to fix a leaky showerhead. He was so smart and funny. Jacob loved to learn. He truly was a little sponge. We stayed close even when he went to New York for college. We talked at least once a week. His graduation day was one of the happiest moments of my life.

"After he graduated, he decided to stay on the East Coast, which broke our hearts, but we understood. He had been offered a great job opportunity at an architecture firm. Jacob loved architecture. He could talk about it for hours. Something I never really thought about or appreciated until he taught me. He showed me how to look at a building. The beautiful details, the coloring, the type of brick or concrete, the ornate features that everyone else took for granted. He loved New York City. It was full of history and splendid old buildings. Jacob would always be telling me about a new building he had walked by. I would just listen and picture the things he was telling me in my head. It was wonderful. He had a gift for words, and I could listen to him all day.

"Soon the phone calls became less frequent. When they did come, they were much shorter and felt hurried. Jacob always had to be somewhere. I tried not to let it bother me. He was in his mid-twenties, in New York, meeting friends, working hard, all of that. Time went on, and we had all planned a trip to New York in the summer to see Jacob and celebrate his twenty-fifth birthday. After we landed at the airport, we took a cab to get settled at the hotel. It was me, my wife, Irene, Abraham, and Rachel. We had planned to all meet up in the hotel lobby at six in the evening, and then head over to a restaurant Jacob had picked out for his birthday. We were all waiting in the lobby when Abraham received a call from Jacob. Abraham said Jacob sounded very stressed and would not be able to join us for dinner as planned. Jacob had to work late again to finish another big project. There was always a big project he was working on. The industry could be very intense, and there was a lot of competition, even within his own office. Abraham told Jacob we would bring him some food and asked him what he wanted.

"After we had dinner, we all went to Jacob's work. Abraham called and told Jacob we were outside. Jacob came down to the street a few minutes later. He looked like a completely different person. He looked so much older. His hair was long, his skin pale, and he was too thin. My beautiful grandson had lost his shiny glow. Mostly he had lost the spark in his eyes. Jacob looked so tired and frail. I wanted to take him home with me and feed him matzo ball soup for a month.

"Jacob gave us all hugs and thanked us for his dinner. We also had brought him a piece of chocolate cake for his dessert and put a candle on it. We told him we would have a real birthday cake tomorrow when he could enjoy it. A few minutes later, Jacob said his goodbyes and went back to work.

"The next few days, we saw Jacob a total of probably eight hours. His work schedule was ridiculous. We all knew he was not sleeping or eating well. When we said our goodbyes, I took him aside to talk.

"I said, 'Jacob, are you okay? We are all worried about you. We want you to come home.' He said, 'Grandpa, yes, I'm fine. It's just a bad week. I'm sorry I couldn't spend more time with you. It meant so much you all came out to visit me. I will be okay. I promise.' Then he grinned that sweet, contagious grin.

"'You need to take care of yourself,' I said. 'You need to meet a nice girl, get married, all that good stuff. Work will always be there, but your life will not.'

"He said, 'Yes, Grandpa. But not all of us want to get married at twenty and have families anymore.' I told him, 'I got it. Just know we love you very much.' And I gave him one last hug.

"I didn't know it would be the last hug I would ever give Jacob. I would have never let go of that kid if I had known that. About six months later, Abraham called to tell me Jacob had died. At first, he would not tell me what happened. He didn't want to tell me over the phone. When Irene and I got to Abraham's house, he had us sit down. We could hear Rachel sobbing from the upstairs bedroom. Jacob had hung himself in his apartment.

"I was in shock. That wasn't possible. My beautiful grandson, dead? It couldn't be true. A parent and grandparent should never outlive the children in their family. Never. What kind of God could have let this happen to my grandson? Our family had always worshipped, prayed, loved God. And this was how he repaid us. I turned my back on God that day. I blamed God, Jacob's boss, the architecture firm, his clients, myself, everyone, for a very long time. My family, friends, the temple—all were gracious and loving to me, but I just didn't want to talk to anyone. Especially God. In Judaism we don't believe in heaven or hell. Loved ones live on in our thoughts and memories. I tried to focus on that, but the memories became too painful sometimes. My son was finally able to convince me to visit Dr. Mike. I was like, who goes by 'Dr. Mike'? What is he, a wannabe Dr. Phil? I was wrong. It was love at first sight. Dr. Mike invited me to the group therapy session about five years ago, and I'm still going strong. Now, I just come for the free food, but it's all good." Sal looked at Mike and smiled.

"I think that is how I got you to come to the first meeting—by promising you free food," Mike said, half laughing.

"That sounds about right," Sal chuckled.

"Okay, Claudia, you are up, if you feel like talking tonight," Mike said compassionately.

"Yeah, I'm okay today," she said. "Well, some of you may know why I love Halloween. It's because it was my dad's favorite holiday. We would dress up, decorate the inside and outside of our house, and eat tons of candy. I still dress up, decorate the house, and eat tons of candy, but it's just not the same. It's lonely and sad without him. My dad gave up his life in order to save mine. We were white water rafting in Colorado when I was on summer break from the eighth grade. I was going into high school that fall, and Dad wanted to take me on a special vacation wherever I wanted. I was really into sports and had always wanted to go rafting. He used to go all of the time when he was younger but hadn't been for a long time.

"After my mom died of cancer when I was seven, neither one of us really wanted to do anything. I don't know what happened, but one day, about a year or so after Mom's death, Dad seemed to snap out of it and wanted to start going places again. His enthusiasm and love made me want to start doing things again too. We started going to baseball games, movies, hiking, all of it. It was a lot of fun. I started connecting with friends at school again and accepting the fact that my dad was both parents now. I was lucky to have such a great dad.

"The second day of our rafting trip, we went out, and the water was a little crazy, but the guide said we should all be okay if we listened to him and followed the safety procedures. He said we would stop if the conditions worsened. About thirty minutes into the trip, the water started getting pretty choppy, and it was hard to control the raft. There were ten of us on the boat. We hit a large rock, and some of us fell into the freezing water. I was trying to keep my head out of the water and started flapping my arms and legs as fast and hard as I could. My dad locked eyes with me as he jumped off the raft. I heard the guide yell, 'No, stay here!' The current was painfully strong and I was having a hard time keeping my head above water. I think I blacked out, because when I woke up, my dad was holding me. He had managed to grab me and was trying to swim with me on him. I felt his body struggle to stay above water. He managed to somehow push me toward a large rock with all of the little strength he had left. He yelled, 'Grab something! Hold on as tight as you can, baby girl! I love you.' Those were the last words I heard my dad say. The current was too strong and took him away from me. They found Dad's body the next day. He had sacrificed his life for mine.

"Somehow, I had managed to grab a small piece of brush sticking out from under the rock, and that saved me. I know I would have died that day if he hadn't come after me. I know it's not the same thing as swallowing pills or whatever, but he knowingly gave up his life for me." Claudia wiped tears away. I noticed a few minutes later that Sal was holding Claudia's hand as they sat silently next to each other. They stayed that way for the rest of the meeting.

I hung around after the meeting to talk to Mike again. I told Beth I would be late so she wouldn't worry. She trusted me that I could drive myself now, but she still liked to get texts or calls when I got home.

Mike and I were finally alone. I had watched him say goodbye to each person. He seemed genuine, and I could see why people trusted him.

"Thanks for meeting with me," I said as he took a seat next to me.

"No problem. Let's continue our conversation. Tell me about Chris." Mike smiled.

"Well, Chris was a fun, loving husband. He loved literature, writing, the beach, cooking." I went on to explain how wonderful Chris was for the next five minutes.

"Awesome. He sounds like a wonderful guy," Mike said. "Now tell me the entire story." He looked me directly in the eyes.

"I don't know what you mean. I told you everything." I got defensive all of a sudden.

"I meant nobody's life is one hundred percent perfect all of the time. What were some of Chris's flaws? Did you ever fight?" Mike asked.

"What? Those are weird questions to ask. He's dead, for God's sake. What does it matter now?" I said, a little louder than I had wanted.

"We tend to put people who died on a pedestal and don't recall the person fully. It's important to remember the good, but I also want you to remember the bad. I want you to overcome the guilt and denial and all of that and someday embrace the acceptance of his death. In order to do this, you need to be completely honest with yourself. Which means remembering everything. It takes time. We often feel they were perfect and that we were the ones that failed them."

"I know it's his fucking fault. I know he was sick. I just thought he was better. He seemed so much better. I don't even know what's true and what's fiction anymore. If I thought he was fine before he killed himself, maybe he was unhappy more times than I knew. Maybe he was unhappy all of his life. Maybe I was just this distraction he liked to have around, and he was incapable of any kind of love at all. He just used me, and then when he got tired of all of it, of me, he decided to jump off a roof. He chose death over me. Is that what you want to hear? That I feel so embarrassed as a person, as a wife, that my husband would rather kill himself than be with me?" I was holding back tears. I didn't want a repeat of last time.

"Stop being selfish," Mike said loudly but gently. "Not everything has to do with you. Chris killing himself had nothing to do with you. That is what you need to understand. He was ill and was able to hide it from his loved ones. It's not your fault. Chris was capable of love, and he loved you. Him killing himself was his decision. It wasn't because he didn't love you anymore or because he never loved anyone. He probably felt alone and scared. He probably thought it was better for everyone if he just left the world. He didn't want you to see his true self and would rather you lived and moved on without him. Remember, people like Chris are not thinking rationally. Their minds are all over the place. They are feeling mixed emotions and many times fighting depression. It's easy for us to judge and just say, 'Get out of bed, take your medication, get over it.' It's not that simple for them. It is literally a chemical imbalance. They have no control over it. It's okay for you to be mad, angry, sad, whatever. Those are all feelings you need to express. Don't just hide behind your emotions and feelings and pretend everything is okay. It's okay to have a bad day here and there. You are grieving. You will always be grieving. My mom died over thirty years ago, and I'm still grieving. I understand it better, and it doesn't hinder my day-to-day life anymore, but it's a process. Embrace your emotions and feelings."

"I don't want any more goddamn emotions or feelings. I'm so tired I could fucking throw *myself* off a friggin' building right now." I was shaking.

"Anger. Now that's a powerful emotion." Mike grinned.

I started to laugh. "You're goddamn right it is."

"Why don't you come out with the group tonight? We're meeting at the new soft-serve place downtown on Fourth."

"Okay, yes, okay. I will go," I said. It came out as a question more than an answer. I had meant to say no, but yes came out instead. I must have felt bad about yelling at Mike, but he called me selfish. Somehow our conservation had lifted some weight off of my shoulders. I felt somewhat human. I felt like I wanted some soft serve. Mike had asked if I wanted to go with him and said he would drive me back, but I opted to drive myself so I could leave from the soft-serve place. Plus, I didn't want to make him drive all the way back to drop me off.

While I was driving, I realized it was my first time on the freeway since Chris had died. It felt weird driving again. Since Chris had died, Beth and Mark had been chauffeuring me around for the most part. As I headed downtown, I started to think about the Turner Building. The building was in the Pasadena area where Chris had grown up, about an hour away from our house, depending on traffic. Martin and Janet still lived in the same house Chris and John had grown up in, which was only a short drive from the Turner Building. When the police initially told me that Chris had died at the Turner Building, it took me a few moments to realize what was Chris's connection with that building. His nanny—or his real mom, he would say—had lived there. Cybil was a widow who'd taken care of Chris and John since they were babies. She would read to them, sing with them, take them to the park, help them with their homework, and take care of them when they were sick. Chris told me he and John never asked for Mom when they needed anything. It was always Cybil. Their mom would sometimes get jealous, but it would quickly pass, and she would just make herself another martini.

Cybil had lived with the family until Chris was a

senior in high school. Unfortunately, Cybil fell ill and eventually diagnosed with stage four bone cancer. His parents purchased a condo in the Turner Building for her to stay, and they paid for nursing care. Cybil had no family of her own and had never had any children besides Chris and John. Chris was angry and felt his parents should have allowed Cybil to stay at their house with the nurses. His parents felt it was best if she had her own space. Chris thought they just didn't want to watch her die and had pushed her out of the only home she had known for almost twenty years.

Chris and John went to see her almost every day after school and on the weekends. If one couldn't make it, the other would go. Neither one of them wanted her to ever feel alone or forgotten. Chris said his parents never came to visit Cybil. They would always tell Chris and John to give Cybil their love, or they would send flowers, but that was it. Chris never forgave them for that.

After Cybil died, Chris's parents rented the condo to some nursing students. We found out that Chris still had a key to the roof, and that was how he'd gained access that day. He'd probably gone to the roof many times before. It was probably a place for him to think, to gain clarity. Chris never told me about the roof. John later told me that they would take Cybil up there to get some sun and fresh air on the days she felt like going outside. Chris probably felt close to Cybil there. Thinking of her spirit with Chris made me happy. I wished I had had the chance to meet Cybil. She sounded like a wonderful woman who made such a huge impact on Chris and John.

I parked and walked over to the soft-serve place. It was bright and loud. People were outside in groups, eating, laughing, having fun. I felt out of place. I saw the group inside. Some already had their soft serve, and others were still in line. I wasn't sure if I should go inside or wait until Mike got there. I wasn't sure if I would fit in, whom I should talk to, or if I should just leave.

All of a sudden, I heard my name. "Kara. Hey, Kara." I turned around and saw Ruben and Sal crossing the street toward me. Crap, I was stuck now.

"Hey," I said, trying to sound upbeat.

"Hi! Glad you could make it. I can't wait to try this soft serve these yahoos keep yapping about," Sal said as he adjusted his hat.

We walked inside and got in line. Jan, Lynn, Elliot, Mary, Efrain, and Frank were inside. They all waved and said hi to me. It wasn't as awkward as I thought it would be. We all met outside and pushed a few plastic tables together. I sat on the end between Sal and Mary. I felt surprisingly safe and calm as we sat and made jokes about the gigantic monstrosity of a sundae Sal had ordered. It was vanilla and chocolate everything, with toppings galore. Everything from M&M's to gummy worms were floating in his Styrofoam cup.

"Oh my God, how have you not had a heart attack yet, old man?" Ruben asked.

Sal smiled away as he kept eating his sundae.

"I'm going to tell Irene, Sal," Mary said jokingly.

"No, no, please. I'm already on egg whites and wheat toast. She says I'm lucky I get any gluten at all now." Sal rolled his eyes. "Whatever the hell gluten is."

We all giggled.

"I tell her, gluten is what makes you full. No one in my day was allergic or sensitive to gluten, eggs, dairy, anything. We were true hard-asses. Not these damn wimps that can't even drink a glass of whole milk without bitching."

"Hey, I'm lactose intolerant," Elliot said as he took a bite of his raspberry sorbet.

"Yeah, my point exactly," Sal quipped.

Everyone laughed.

Mike came up to our tables. "Hey, everyone."

"We saved you a seat," Elliot said as he pointed to the empty spot next to him.

"Nice, thanks," Mike said as he sat down.

"Aren't you going to get some soft serve, Mike?" Frank asked.

"No, I'm trying to watch my sugar and dairy intake."

"Oy vey!" Sal shouted as he pumped his arms in the air.

We sat and chatted for about an hour. It was weird to see everyone outside of that fluorescent-lit classroom. We met twice a month, but they tried to do an extracurricular activity as a group at least once a month as well.

"What are everyone's plans for the weekend?" Mike asked as he looked around the table.

"Lynn and I are having a garage sale. We have been cleaning and trying to get rid of some stuff around the house," Jan said as she smiled at Lynn. I hadn't realized Jan and Lynn were sisters until I overheard Elliot talking to Jan one time. Jan was really sweet—often too perky, but such a caring person. Lynn could be such a downer. That was funny coming from me because I was a definite downer. Jan and Lynn didn't talk much in group, but I heard that their sister died about year ago. They had all been very close. The sisters were not blood related, but they'd all spent several years together in a foster home. Lynn and Jan were probably a few years older than I. From what I could gather, their late sister Natalie had been a gentle but tormented girl. Her family life prior to the decent foster home the three of them shared had been pretty horrific. Natalie was in therapy many years trying to overcome her past. Unfortunately, the damage was done, and Natalie killed herself by leaving the car on in the closed garage three days after her forty-third birthday. Carbon monoxide poisoning. Lynn had been the one that found her. Natalie had been living with Lynn and Jan off and on because it was hard for her to keep a stable job. Natalie loved animals and worked in several different veterinarian clinics and dog-grooming businesses, but it was hard for her to maintain a routine.

I wondered how Lynn and Jan were before Natalie's death. Maybe Lynn had been more outgoing and Jan more of a realist. Who knew? This life-after-death thing definitely changed you. I had no idea who I was anymore. I looked in the mirror and saw a depressed, old crazy person. If myself from four months ago saw myself now, she would not have even recognized her.

Apparently, I'd zoned out during the weekend conversations. Then Elliot asked me, "Hey, Kara, what are you doing this weekend?"

"Um, not much. I need to catch up on some work. I'm going back to the office on Monday."

"What do you do?" Ruben asked.

"I'm a paralegal at a civil litigation firm downtown. I've been working from home since…since, um, the, you know, Chris, and my boss has been understanding, but it's time to get back." I felt my face turning red.

"Are you nervous?" Elliot asked innocently.

"A little. I haven't seen some of my co-workers since before, you know, or some were at the funeral. I just don't want everyone staring at me and feeling sorry for me like I'm a freak or something." I couldn't believe what I was saying out loud to this group of people I barely knew.

"The first week is the hardest," Mary said sweetly. "Once you get past it, everything kind of falls back into routine. That is the only good thing about work. It does keep your mind occupied. I went back to work two weeks after Travis passed. It was difficult, and I just wanted to sit home and cry all day, but I also needed to pay the bills. It will help."

"We are all freaks," Jensen interjected. "If anyone gives you a hard time, just let us know, and we'll come by and really give them something to stare at."

The group cheered.

"Damn right!" Efrain yelled.

"Kara, don't feel like you are an outsider," Mike said.

"These people, your co-workers, they are your friends. They care about you. Sometimes people don't know what to say or how to act around a person who's lost someone. Especially a person who's lost someone in a sudden, unexpected way. Just be open and honest with them." He nodded and smiled.

"You mean someone that offed themselves, Doc?" Efrain asked sarcastically.

"Efrain, you know that is not the best way to describe it."

"It is what it is. Call it like we see it," Lynn said.

"Oh, Lynn," Jan said in a disappointed tone.

"Okay, okay. Call it whatever you want, but my point is, people are here for Kara, and for all of us. We just need to give people a chance. All of us remember what it was like to go back to work, school, whatever after the death of a loved one. It's hard taking that step back into our old routine, into what our life used to be. We have to make a new path with what we are left with."

"Making lemonade out of lemons," Sal said as he scraped the bottom of his bowl for the last few bites of soft serve.

The group dispersed about an hour later. I felt exhausted from sharing all of those damn feelings. Mike had told me before we left to call or text him if I had any issues at work or just wanted to talk. I thanked him. Sal and Ruben walked me back to my car. We said our goodbyes and that we would see each other at the next meeting. Sal gently touched my arm and said, "It'll be okay, kid. You're strong and will get through this." I smiled and thanked him. Such simple words, but coming from Sal, they felt much deeper. Like a dad giving his daughter words of encouragement and love before her wedding day. Not my dad, but some other dad.

CHAPTER 10

Sunday night came and went so fast. I can't believe it had been over eight weeks since I'd last seen Chris. Time had been so inconsistent. Some days went by quickly, and others just dragged on. My mom, Beth, Dawn, and John had all called to check on me and to wish me well at work tomorrow. I started going through my closet to pick out an outfit. I was having flashbacks from when I was trying to decide on clothes for my first day of work at the firm almost five years ago. I already had butterflies in my stomach thinking about Monday. Every time I went into our closet, I would avoid looking toward the right because that was where most of Chris's clothes were. A couple of weeks ago, Beth had asked me if I wanted to go through his stuff. I told her I wasn't ready, and she understood. Beth told me to let her know, and she would help me with anything. I didn't know if I would ever be ready to go through Chris's things. That would mean he was really gone and not coming back. For now, I could still pretend he was on an extended business trip, and I was just counting the days until he came home. I liked that feeling, and I wasn't ready to give that up yet.

When I was doing laundry a few weeks ago, I realized it was all mine. None of Chris's shirts, pants, underwear, or socks accompanied my clothes in the washer. The load of clothes looked so small all by themselves, just sitting in the washing machine. I remembered feeling sad for my clothes. In a weird way, I sensed my clothes missed his clothes. They had been washed, dried, and folded together for years. Now they were probably wondering where his clothes had gone. Chris's poor clothes were probably asking, "Where is that guy with the sweet sense of humor and nice cologne? Is he ever going to come back and put me on again?" No! Nope, he was never going to put on his old, broken-in pair of blue jeans. Nor would he ever wear that blue shirt I had bought him for Christmas last year. All of it was pointless. His possessions were now just useless space for a man who'd left us. A man who would never return.

I sat on the hardwood floor, my back against the front of the bed, and started bawling. After a few minutes, I was able to calm myself down. I just sat in the same spot, staring at the closet. My side of the closet was a mess. I had clothes everywhere. My shirts and dresses hung over the door frame and on the doorknobs. Chris's side of the closet remained still and untouched. I had this indescribable feeling to run and just hold onto his clothes, but I couldn't get my legs to take me over there. I just continued to stare. Luckily, I had already made peace with his shampoo and other toiletries in the bathroom. I didn't bother them as long as they didn't try and remind me of Chris. We had a mutual understanding to stay away from each other. It was the same deal I had with Chris's wedding ring. I knew some people wore their loved one's rings on their own fingers or put the ring on a necklace, but it I couldn't do it. When Detective Jackson had returned Chris's watch, wedding ring, and what was left of his wallet to me, I immediately put everything in the top drawer of his nightstand. They were all too painful to look at, so I chose to ignore them.

After a few more tears and thoughts of the past, I finally forced myself up and decided on the gray suit with the wine-colored top. Chris had always liked that blouse on me. I went to bed thinking about Chris and wondering what he was doing right now while he was away on his business trip.

My alarm yelled at me, and I rolled out of bed. I hadn't been up at 6:00 a.m. on purpose for a while. The last time must have been the day Chris died. I was usually up by 6:15 a.m. during the week. Chris had not been a morning person, so he tried to avoid teaching the eight o'clock classes as much as possible. He was usually up by the time I left at seven to give me a kiss and get a fresh cup of coffee.

Thursday, January 25, had been the same as every morning. I woke up around six and got ready for work. Chris came downstairs about five minutes before I had to leave and grabbed a cup of coffee. The last time I saw Chris alive, he was wearing his sweatpants and old Star

Wars T-shirt. I was wearing the blue suit with the white blouse I had just bought over the weekend. I thought it might have been a little too low cut. Chris had laughed and called me a granny. It was a running joke with our family because I did prefer to wear sweaters and pants rather than skirts and tank tops. He was making himself a bowl of Cocoa Pebbles on my way out.

"Hey, what are you making me for dinner?" I asked lovingly.

"Um, I feel like it might be a Cocoa Pebbles kind of night," Chris chuckled as he took a big bite of his favorite cereal.

"You're going to turn into a Cocoa Pebble, eating that all of the time," I teased.

"I hope so. That would be awesome." Chris smiled as he walked over and kissed me goodbye.

"Love you," he said softly.

"Love you too," I said, rushing out the door.

I often wondered if Chris knew those were the last moments we would share. Had he been planning his suicide while watching cartoons and eating Cocoa Pebbles that morning? Had he been planning it for longer? Or had it been a last-minute type of thing where something had triggered him to jump off a ledge that night?

I wished I could go back to that day. I should have never ended our kiss. I could have suggested we stay in bed all day, watch TV, and eat ice cream. I wished I had called Chris that afternoon instead of texting him. My last text to Chris was around twelve thirty. There was a stray cat that hung around my office building, so some of us would feed her. I sent him a picture of the kitty, whose name was Sugar, with a heart emoji. We both were animal lovers. Chris was more of a dog person and I was more of a cat person, but we loved both. We had adopted a cat when we lived in Washington. The Humane Society had estimated he was about one year old. Unfortunately, about four years after we adopted him, he was run over by a car. It broke our hearts. We loved Snuggles, aka Mr. Snuggles, so much. We had talked about getting another cat or a dog or both, but we never did.

Chris had replied back to my text with a heart emoji, and that was it. I got busy again with work, and I knew he was probably still at school, working. I later found out the detectives had traced Chris's steps that day. After I left the house, he'd gone to work and taught his ten o'clock class. He'd spoken with a few students after class who were asking questions about their upcoming research paper, and then he'd gone to his office. The students told the police there had been nothing unusual about Chris's behavior. He'd been well liked by students and professors on campus. Many of them had attended his funeral and even written me letters and sent flowers.

Dr. Warren, a fellow English professor, was suspected to have been the last person to speak to Chris on campus. Her office was right next his. She was unlocking her office door as Chris was locking his door to leave. She said hello, and he returned a quick hello as he rushed by her. She said he'd left in a hurry and estimated the time was around 2:30 p.m. From a receipt found in Chris's wallet, the police said Chris had purchased a bottle of Scotch at a liquor store near the Turner Building at 3:57 p.m. Investigators estimated that Chris had arrived at the Turner Building around 4:15 p.m. No one noticed Chris enter the building. He had keys and didn't cause any disturbance when he walked in. The nursing students renting Cybil's apartment were interviewed, and neither one of them saw Chris that day. The detectives said he'd probably gone straight to the rooftop. All Chris left was a near-empty bottle of Scotch sitting on the ledge next to his key chain with car keys. The key chain had been a gift from me after Chris had accepted his teaching position at the university. I remembered giving it to him the night before we moved back to California. We'd had sangria and fish tacos at our favorite place down the street from our apartment building. After the delicious meal, we walked home, holding hands in the rain, and came back upstairs to finish packing. I told him I was very proud of him and excited for this next chapter in our lives as I handed him the little wrapped box. Chris's eyes lit up like he'd just won the Publisher's Clearing House sweepstakes. I smiled as I watched him carefully open the gift. I would never forget that look of happiness that melted over his face. He thanked me profusely and immediately put his keys on the new key ring. It wasn't much, because we didn't have a lot of money, but Chris loved it. The key chain was silver plated and had his initials on it. A key chain, something so small, so insignificant, was now something I thought about all of the time. Maybe Chris had left it on the roof because he didn't want the police to have to give me a blood-soaked key chain from his pocket. I pictured Chris going through his last day with that dumb key chain in his pocket. What were his thoughts, whom did he speak with, did someone or something set him off that day? I also wondered why he'd left the key chain on the roof, but jumped with his wallet, wedding ring, and watch still on him. Sometimes these things were all I could think about and plagued my thoughts for hours at a time. I told this to Beth once. She told me to stop being morbid and that I shouldn't think about things like that.

I remembered I was in the kitchen when I got the call from Detective Jackson. It was around 7:30 p.m., and I had just gotten home from work a few minutes prior. I had parked my car in the garage, wondering where Chris was, but thinking he might have gotten caught up talking with a student or colleague, or he'd lost track of time while researching or writing in his office. I was getting ready to grab some crackers to snack on before I changed my clothes and called Chris to see what the ETA was on dinner.

I didn't recognize the phone number calling my cell.

"Hello," I answered.

"Hello, is this Kara McKay?" an unfamiliar male voice asked.

"Yes."

"Mrs. McKay, I'm Detective Jackson. There has been an incident, and…"

"Oh my God, is it Chris? Is he okay? Where is Chris?" I shouted.

"I'm on my way over to your home right now. Are you at home?" Detective Jackson asked.

"Yes, I'm here."

"Okay, I'll be at your house in about twenty minutes," Detective Jackson said.

"Twenty minutes? I can just meet you. Please tell me what's wrong. Where is Chris?" I pleaded.

"Mrs. McKay, we can talk when I get there. I'll see you soon. Don't go anywhere," Detective Jackson said politely but firmly.

"Okay." I hung up and called Beth. I don't know what I said, or if anything made sense, but Beth and Mark came over right away. Fortunately, they lived only minutes away. They left the twins at a neighbor's house and headed right over.

"What did the police officer say exactly?" Beth asked. She was trying to sound calm, but I could tell she was scared as hell, like I was.

"I don't know. Something about an incident. He wouldn't answer my questions."

"Maybe it was just a car accident. Some stupid jerk rear-ended Chris or something. I'm sure it will be okay, you guys," Mark said.

"Yeah, I'm sure it's fine, Kare," Beth said as she tried to crack a smile.

"I've been trying to call Chris's cell phone, but the damn thing keeps going straight to voicemail," I said.

A few minutes after Beth and Mark arrived at the

house, we heard the doorbell. All three of us jumped and ran to answer the door. A tall man in a tan suit was waiting for us.

"Mrs. McKay?" he asked.

"Yes, what's going on? Where's Chris?" I tried to stay calm but felt like I was going to explode.

"Please come in." Mark invited Detective Jackson inside.

"I'm Detective Jackson." He flashed his police badge. "Are you all family?"

"Yes, I'm Mark Cruz, and this is my wife, Beth, Kara's sister."

I couldn't hold it together any longer. "Now that we all know who we are, what the fuck is going on? *Where is Chris?*"

"I'm sorry, Mrs. McKay, but Chris has passed away," Detective Jackson said solemnly.

Silence followed for a few seconds while we all processed what Detective Jackson had said.

"Oh my God, that's not possible. He was alive this morning. He had breakfast, probably went for a run, went to work. He is fine," I said as I fought back the tears. "No, Chris can't be...I just saw him twelve hours ago."

"I'm sorry, Mrs. McKay." Detective Jackson motioned for us to sit down. We all complied.

"No, no, no, this has to be a mistake." I started to sob.

"What happened? How did this happen?" Mark asked. Beth was holding me next to her. I could feel myself shaking in her arms. Or was that her shaking? I couldn't tell.

"Self-inflicted. We received numerous calls that a man matching Chris's description jumped from the Turner Building at approximately 6:03 p.m. Mr. McKay was found and pronounced dead at the scene. He had his ID and wallet on him."

"I don't believe it. It can't be. It can't be Chris. He was okay. He was doing okay. I know he was."

"Mrs. McKay, was your husband upset? Has he attempted suicide before?"

"No, never. He was doing better. He was on his meds. We were starting to plan a trip in June for our wedding anniversary. I…I…I'm gonna be sick." I ran to the restroom and threw up. I held my head in the toilet, trying to catch my breath. I got up and washed my hands and face, and Beth walked in. I could tell she had been crying too.

"Oh my God, Kare, I'm so sorry."

"I know, I know." We just held each other. A few moments passed, and then we somehow mustered the strength to return to the living room.

"Mrs. McKay, do you have friends or family you can stay with tonight?"

"Yes, she can stay with us," Beth said quickly.

"Okay, good. I'm leaving you my card and the card of a therapist who helps families through these situations." Detective Jackson left the business cards on the coffee table as he began to stand up. "Is there someone else I can call for you, Ms. McKay? Did Mr. McKay have any other family?"

"Oh my God, yes—John. His brother, John, and he were very close…No, I should call him, and he can call their parents." I started panicking. What was I going to say John? There were no words.

"I hate to ask this, but do you mind if I take a look through Mr. McKay's belongings? His room, his office?" Detective Jackson asked.

The doorbell rang. Who the hell could that be? Who knew what happened already?

Detective Jackson must have read my mind. "Oh, that must be my partner, Detective Raines. Do you mind if I answer the door?" I shook my head.

Detective Raines entered and made his introductions.

"Mrs. McKay, do you mind if we look around?" Detective Jackson asked again.

"Is that absolutely necessary?" Beth asked, sounding like an overprotective mother.

"Well, sometimes we will find something that will give us more answers. We didn't find a note at the scene and just wanted to look around here and his office at work," Detective Jackson explained.

"Yes, go ahead," I said as I looked out toward the patio. It was raining. When had that happened? Today had been a beautiful day. It had probably gotten up to about sixty degrees, blue skies, gorgeous. Then I thought about Chris's blood on the street. I imagined his blood pouring into the storm drains. I couldn't catch my breath. I needed some air. I quickly stood up, opened the door to the back patio, and went outside. The rain felt cool and refreshing on my burning skin, but I still felt like I was on fire. I took a deep breath and let it out as I sat down on the concrete and wept.

CHAPTER 11

W*ake up, Kara! Wake up from this horrible nightmare. This isn't happening. Chris is in bed next to you. Wake up!*

The day after Chris's death, I woke up and found myself on the couch in the living room. The sun was up, but it still felt early. What time was it? What day was it? What a crazy nightmare. I sat up and noticed my hair was damp, and I was wearing the same clothes I'd had on in my dream. I looked over and saw Beth on the couch across from me. She was in the same clothes from last night too. Two business cards sat on the coffee table. I walked over slowly and picked them up. One was for Detective Jackson, and the other was for a Dr. Evelyn Sinclair. No, it wasn't a nightmare. Or was I still in the nightmare and just couldn't get out?

Beth heard my screaming and jumped off the couch. She came over and just held me. She walked me over to the couch, gently sat me down next to her, and we cuddled with the blanket. We didn't say anything. We both just cried and held each other until Mark walked in.

"Hey, I got the boys off to day care. Brought some coffee and donuts if anyone wants anything." Mark put everything on the kitchen table and started assembling the coffee.

Beth kissed me on the head and then walked toward the kitchen. She grabbed a cup of coffee and poured in a splash of milk, just the way I liked it. She brought the coffee and a chocolate donut and laid them on the coffee table in front of me.

"I'm okay," I said.

"Kare, you need to eat and drink something."

"I will. I promise…Fuck. I never called John last night." I started looking for my cell phone. "Crap, does Mom know? Does work know?" I asked out loud.

"Kare, I called John last night. I thought he should know and let their parents know. He was going to drive down from Santa Barbara last night, and Detective Jackson was going to reach out to him too. I didn't want to wake you. You were pretty hysterical, and we had finally gotten you down. You needed your rest," Beth said tenderly.

"I called your work this morning, Kare. I spoke with Syd, and he is so sorry. He said he will call you later this week to check on you, but don't worry about anything right now. I also called the English department and spoke with the dean. He had heard about Chris on social media last night and was very sorry. He said Chris was an excellent professor and friend to everyone and will be missed." Mark spoke softly, as if he were talking to the twins.

"What social media?" I asked.

"I think one of the students at the college found out somehow, and then it got around pretty quickly that it was Chris," Mark said, shaking his head.

I jumped up from the couch and grabbed the newspaper Mark had left on the kitchen table. I skimmed the front page, and at the bottom was a picture of Chris, the one from the college's website. He was wearing his gray suit with black shirt and tie. The college had taken that photo of Chris when he'd first started teaching there. I remembered him telling me he regretted wearing that suit because it reminded him of his father. The article beneath the photo was entitled "Professor Leaps to Death." The article said Chris had "jumped to his death in an apparent suicide. The scene caused the street to be blocked off for hours, causing major traffic delays."

"What the fuck is this?" I asked out loud to myself.

"Kara, don't!" Beth begged. She got up and tried to grab the paper from me.

"No, wait…it says, 'Mr. McKay is survived by his loving wife, brother, and parents.' Wow, how does the newspaper get all of this crap so fast?" I threw the paper across the table.

"Don't think about that, Kare. Listen, I spoke with Mom, and she is going to come by this morning. She wanted me to tell you she loves you. I also spoke with Dawn, and she said the same thing." Beth found my cell phone in the couch and handed it to me.

I looked at my phone. Eleven missed calls, thirteen missed texts. I was already feeling overwhelmed, and I hadn't even opened my messages yet.

"I'm going to take a shower." I ran upstairs to our bedroom. Our bedroom. I threw my clothes off as fast as I could and jumped in the shower. It felt quiet and safe in the shower. No one could hear me weeping and cursing. The water eventually started turning cold and forced me to leave. If the water had stayed warm, I probably would have hidden in there forever.

I dried off and threw on some sweatpants. I saw Chris's Star Wars T-shirt on the bed. It was old and gray but still Chris's favorite shirt. The soft cotton embraced my body like a cozy blanket after a long day. I could faintly smell Chris's cologne still lingering on his shirt, and I started to cry. I lay on Chris's side of the bed, hoping it would warm me up, but it just felt cold and stiff. I must have cried myself to sleep because when I opened my eyes again, they felt extremely dry and wet at the same time. There was barely any light in the room because the sun was disappearing outside. I wondered if Beth and Mark were still here. I went downstairs to investigate. Beth was sitting at the kitchen table, working on her laptop.

"Hey there. How are you feeling? Did you get some rest?" Beth asked.

Before I even answered, my mom appeared from the patio.

"Oh, sweetie," Mom said. I ran over to her before she completely made it inside the house. We hugged and sat down next to each other on the couch.

"I'm so sorry, baby girl," Mom said as she burst into tears. Then she whispered, "Dawn and Jason came by a little while ago. They wanted to tell you they are thinking of you."

The doorbell rang. Beth answered, and it was John. I stood up, and we hugged. After the polite chitchat with my mom and Beth, John asked if we could speak alone. We went into Chris's office.

"Kare, I'm so sorry. I can't believe this. I'm still in shock," John said as he paced back and forth.

"I know, I know. It doesn't seem real," I said quietly.

"I talked to my parents, and they want to help with the funeral arrangements. I told Mom we would call her later."

"John, you know Chris wouldn't want anything from your parents. Not even for funeral arrangements," I said sternly. I wasn't mad, but I didn't want his parents involved.

"Kare, Chris was their son. I know they didn't get along all of the time, but I can't tell my grieving mother no if she wants to help out with the funeral arrangements. No mother should ever have to bury a child. Plus, funerals are expensive," John said.

"We have money. We aren't rich like you or your parents, but we are fine," I said defensively.

"Kare, that's not what I meant. Chris's life insurance will not kick in because his death was suicide. Mom doesn't know how to express her love, so paying for the funeral is the best way she knows how."

"I know. Whatever. I don't care," I said like a pouting child.

"Okay, I'm sorry. I don't want to be caught in the middle. I have no idea what the hell I'm doing." John stood glaring through the glass patio door, trying not to let me see him cry.

"Why would he do this, John?" I asked. "He seemed so much better after the clinic last summer. He was happy, or at least I thought he was happy. He was taking his meds, teaching, writing…it all felt good again." I hoped that John would know all of the answers.

"I don't know, Kare. The last time I spoke with Chris was a few weeks ago. He admitted the meds were making him tired, and he was still having a hard time focusing. Chris was trying. He really wanted to make it work."

"Why didn't he tell me any of this? Am I so fucking blind I didn't even notice?" I yelled at myself.

"He loved you. He didn't want you to worry." John turned and looked at me sitting on the couch.

"Maybe if I had been better at knowing he was faking, he would still be here, John."

John walked over to the couch. "He fooled all of us. I didn't think it was that bad either. If I thought it was, I would have told you…" His voice trailed off.

"There's something I do need to tell you," John said gently as he took a seat next to me and looked down at the floor. "The cops were asking me questions and told me you said Chris had never tried to commit suicide before." John paused for a minute. "Well, that's not entirely true." He looked directly in my eyes now.

I just stared at him, dumbfounded. "What are you

talking about? Chris never tried this before. I would have known." My face started to feel warm again.

"No, it was before you guys met. Chris was around fourteen. He had been struggling in school, fighting depression, puberty, hormones, all of that crap. He was seeing therapists, taking all kinds of meds, drinking. My parents were out of town, and I came home from school late because I had soccer practice. My friend's parents dropped me off at home. I knew Cybil was picking her sister up from the airport that afternoon, so that's why I had hitched a ride from them. I knew Chris was home because the lights were on in the house. Music was blasting from his room. I tried knocking on his door, but no one answered. The door was locked and I felt that something must have been wrong. I finally was able to kick open the door and found Chris lying on the floor in a pool of vomit. He had swallowed a bunch of those damn prescription pills, along with some of mom's Vicodin and Dad's Scotch. I called 911, and they were able to pump his stomach at the hospital. Cybil and her sister met me in the emergency room. We called Mom and Dad, and they came back from their vacation the next day. Chris was gone for a few weeks. I wasn't sure where they put him. When he came back home, he was a zombie. I know now they probably had him doped up on so much medication that he couldn't even think straight. It was bad for a while, but then by the summer, things seemed to have calmed down. I just thought you should know in case the police bring it up again or you hear it from someone else." John grabbed my hand and squeezed.

We sat in silence for several minutes while I tried to process what John had just told me. Why did Chris never tell me? Did I even know him at all? I felt like such a fool. John must have felt my thoughts wandering and suggested we call his parents. They sounded as bad as I felt. We discussed the funeral arrangements. It was more of Janet and John discussing, while Martin and I just listened. That was fine with me at this point. I was still trying to come to terms with what John had just told me.

After the phone call, John hugged us all goodbye, and said he would drop by again tomorrow. I walked outside and sat on the back patio. I couldn't breathe in that damn house anymore. Not only had Chris still been struggling, but I was so dumb I hadn't even seen it. He should have been a fucking Academy Award–winning actor, or I must have been the most clueless wife on the goddamn planet. What else was he not telling me? Now I wondered what other secrets he might have hidden from me. Who was this man I was in love with and married to for over fourteen years? Was I in love with someone else? Some other man that Chris had made up. The man I thought I married would not have kept all of these secrets from me.

It was now completely dark outside. I could sense Beth cooking something in the kitchen, and it smelled delicious. A few minutes later, we sat down to enjoy Beth's homemade pot roast. I ate most of everything, in between downing water like I was on a summer hike in Death Valley. I couldn't remember the last time I ate or drank anything. Probably yesterday, I thought. I didn't even hear the front doorbell ring. Beth quickly ran over to the door and let Detective Jackson and Detective Raines inside.

"Hi, Mrs. McKay. We're sorry to bother you. We just had some more information for you," Detective Raines said politely.

"Mrs. McKay, we went to Chris's school and to his office. We found three letters, one addressed to you, one to his brother, and one to his parents." Detective Jackson spoke as if he were ordering a Coke with his sandwich at the deli counter. He probably had gone through this routine many times in his profession. He handed me an envelope with my name on it. I immediately recognized Chris's handwriting and braced myself.

"We will pass along the other notes, Mrs. McKay. If there is anything you need, feel free to contact our office." Detective Raines tipped his hat. I thanked them, and they were on their way. Probably onto the next horrific life event they had to tell someone about. Chris was probably just one of many people that had died yesterday. Chris had just celebrated his thirty-eighth birthday on January 7. We had gone out to dinner to his favorite sushi place that night. At home, I wrote "Happy Birthday, C!!" on his delicious bakery-made cherry pie. I lit eight candles on the birthday pie and sung a horrible rendition of "Happy Birthday." He closed his eyes, made a wish, and blew out his candles. We pulled out two forks and ate pie directly from the pan and finished a bottle of wine. Chris was careful and only had his allotted one glass of alcohol on special occasions or sometimes on the weekend. Compromise. If I had known it was his last birthday, I would have let him drink the whole goddamn bottle himself. I often thought about what he'd wished for when he blew out his candles that night.

CHAPTER 12

I arrived at the office a little earlier than normal to ensure I settled in at my desk before anyone noticed. After being absent for over two months, I found the office looked completely the same. Life went on without me and Chris. Syd, one of the partners I worked for, was already in his office. I went into his office, and we chatted for a few minutes. First it was friendly small talk, and then he told me how sorry he was to hear about Chris. I thanked him for the flowers and for attending the funeral. Fortunately, I was able to maneuver myself out of his office before I started to lose it. I didn't want to cry. Not today. Not in front of my co-workers.

The day was full of friendly hellos and sorrys. Mike was right. It seemed difficult for my friends and co-workers to find the words to say, and they truly did want to just be kind. I appreciated it. Mike texted me around noon and said he hoped my day was going well. He also offered to chat if needed. I texted him back I was fine, but thanked him for checking in. I also received texts from Mom, Beth, Dawn, John, and I think all of the people in the COPE group, even Lynn. I had given my phone number to Jan to add to the group list a few weeks ago. She said the group liked to contact one another for encouragement and sometimes plan activities via text. Sal sent a meme with a cat chasing a mouse that said, "You Got This." It made me laugh. Some of the others chimed in with their own cliché memes, and it was pretty hilarious. It helped pass the afternoon and make it through my first day back to work.

I saw Sugar, the stray cat who hung around the office, at lunchtime, and she made me smile but also tear up a bit. I hadn't seen her since the day Chris died. Sugar must have sensed I needed the love because she walked right over and nuzzled my legs. I spent the rest of my lunch hour just petting her and talking to her. I thought about Sugar the rest of the afternoon and finally made the decision to take her home with me. I used a blanket I kept in the trunk to sweep her up and put her in the back seat of my car. Sugar seemed content until the car started to move. I drove home and carefully put her down on the kitchen floor. I fumbled through the cabinets and found a can of tuna I immediately opened for her. She ate the entire can pretty quickly and then ran under the couch.

My decision to take Sugar home had been impulsive. I had absolutely no supplies for her, so I grabbed my purse to venture out to the pet store. I laughed as I pictured myself gradually turning into of those ladies who puts a leash on their cat or pushes them in a stroller. I must have looked clueless staring at the cat products, intently reading cat food labels, and going back and forth between aisles, because I had two separate store employees come ask if I needed help with anything. I finally picked out the essentials, plus a half-dozen cat toys, and headed back home. I smiled as I grabbed the bags and went into the house. I was excited for Sugar to see all of her new stuff.

I methodically placed her food and water dishes, blanket, bed, and toys throughout the kitchen and living room, but she still stayed under the couch. Even though I couldn't see her, it was comforting to know Sugar was here. I was talking to her about my day and how glad I was she was here with me. I found myself telling Sugar about her daddy, Chris. He was the best daddy, and he was sorry he never got to meet her. He'd loved pictures of her I'd texted him over the past few months and thought she was a very pretty kitty. I told Sugar about how Chris was a dog lover, but underneath was a serious cat lover.

I felt my stomach growling and decided to eat a bowl of cereal. I looked at the top of the fridge where we kept all of the cereal boxes. All that was left was a box of Cheerios and a box of Cocoa Pebbles. I stared at the boxes for a while and finally grabbed the Cocoa Pebbles. I shook the box, and it was about half full. I got the milk out of the fridge and made my dinner. I then sat on the couch, turned on the television to binge-watch *Law and Order*, and opened a bottle of wine. I took a large bite of Cocoa Pebbles, and it felt like chewing rocks. What the hell? Damn you, Chris, and these damn Cocoa Pebbles! I laughed to myself. I threw out my bowl of stale chocolate goodness and refilled the bowl with Cheerios. I carefully put the box of Cocoa Pebbles back on top of the fridge.

I fell asleep about an hour later and woke up just before 3:00 a.m. I was lying on the couch, *Law and Order* was still playing, and Sugar was at my feet, snoozing away. My cell phone was digging into my side. I set my alarm and turned over to go back to sleep. I was careful not to wake Sugar because she looked so peaceful. She was home.

Several Saturdays later, around one in the morning, I was watching *Law and Order* reruns again with Sugar. My cell phone rang, and it startled both of us. The pack of Twizzlers sitting on my chest fell to the ground. I quickly answered my phone, but before I could say hello, Jason shouted, "Matty is coming! We just got to the hospital."

"Okay, I'm on my way!" I yelled back at him and hung up the phone. I leaped off the couch, ran to the bedroom to put on some decent clothes, and was out the door within five minutes.

I arrived at the hospital and was directed to the waiting room. I wanted to call Beth, but I didn't want to wake her, so I texted her. A few hours later, Jason came out to the waiting room and said Dawn had delivered baby Matty. He said both mom and baby girl were doing great. We hugged and I started to cry. I couldn't remember the last time I had cried for something joyous.

"They're just settling Dawn and Matty into a room,

and then we can go see them in a few minutes. I need to call my parents."

The smile on Jason's face was bigger than I had ever seen it. He was definitely a proud father. His parents lived in Ohio. They had been planning on being here for the baby's birth, but Matty decided to make her appearance early.

About thirty minutes later, I finally was able to see Dawn and meet Matty. Matty was adorable! Her eyes were shut, and she was just lying calmly on Dawn. Poor Dawn and Matty looked exhausted, but they were both glowing. I had never seen Dawn look so beautiful. Jason came in and sat on the edge of the bed. I sat in a chair near the bed.

"Can we tell her?" Dawn asked Jason like a child waiting to tell a secret.

"Yes, sure." Jason smiled and looked at me with a big grin on his face.

"Oh my God, you're making me nervous," I said as I sat up in my chair.

"Well, first, we obviously want you to be Matty's godmother. If that's okay with you?" Dawn asked, already knowing the answer.

"Yes! Yes! Of course, yes!" I jumped from the chair and hugged them both.

"That's not all," Jason said like a gameshow host waiting to reveal another surprise.

"What? You guys are too much!" I was trying to think what else it could possibly be. I was hoping I would have the privilege of being Matty's godmother. That in itself was such a wonderful gift. I knew it was a major decision for parents to make, and given where my head had been lately, I would have had second thoughts about myself. I was thrilled they still had faith in me.

"Matilda's full name is going to be Matilda Chris Josephson." Dawn paused for a minute to wipe her eyes. "We want to remember Chris in a special way, and Matilda can have a piece of Chris with her always."

My tears fell swiftly. Dawn and Jason's gesture of love and remembrance was beyond heartfelt. Words could not express the deep emotions I was feeling at that moment.

"That's so beautiful. You guys are the best. I'm honored. Chris would be so touched." We hugged again.

After another hour of baby gawking, we said our goodbyes. I promised Dawn I would check in on them later. I stepped onto the elevator, still coming down off the high from the news Dawn and Jason had just shared with me, and I recognized a familiar face.

"Hi there," Ruben said. He looked as surprised as I probably did. I immediately noticed he was wearing a police uniform.

"Hi! I didn't know you are a cop," I said, trying not to sound like a moron.

"Oh no, I don't really tell everyone. I usually just say I work for the city. When people find out I'm a cop, they usually either try and be my best friend to get out of parking tickets, or they hate me and avoid me." Ruben laughed awkwardly.

"No, I get it."

"Oh yeah, you work for lawyers. You totally get it."

We both laughed. The elevator stopped and we walked outside.

"Is everything okay?" Ruben asked as he motioned toward the hospital.

"Oh yeah, my best friend just had a baby."

"Wow, congrats!"

"Thanks. She's a cutie. What about you? Are you chasing a criminal or something?"

"No, no. I'm off duty. I didn't have a chance to change into my street clothes before I came over. My mom has pneumonia and was admitted yesterday."

"Oh no, I'm sorry."

"Thanks. She's doing better. She is pretty out of it. I think they have her on a lot of different antibiotics, inhalers, you know. My dad, me, my aunts, uncles, cousins, we are all taking turns being here."

"Nice, that is so sweet. Sounds like you have a very loving and close family."

"Yeah, they are pretty special."

"That's great."

"Hey, do you need a ride home or anything?" Ruben asked politely.

"No, I have my car, but thanks. Although, I've always wanted to ride in a police car." I laughed at my own dumb joke.

"Aw, sorry, just my jalopy. The police car is at the station."

"Darn." I smiled.

"I was going to grab some breakfast. Are you hungry?"

Ruben asked. He must have seen the hesitation on my face. "Rain check. We can go some other time," Ruben said as he started to walk away.

"Oh no, yeah, that sounds good. I'm pretty hungry." He was nice, and I shouldn't be rude. We decided to walk a block over to a well-known twenty-four-hour diner.

"I love these places," Ruben said as he opened the door for me.

"I don't think I have ever heard someone talk about diners that way before." I laughed. We sat down and ordered coffee.

"No, think about it. These places are the heart and soul of the city. Open twenty-four hours a day. Serving all sorts of people all times of day. People that work at these places have some crazy stories. And that's saying a lot, coming from a cop. We have some pretty amazing stories ourselves." Ruben smiled.

"I bet."

We talked about our families, growing up in the area, working too much, and life moving by so fast.

"So, you and Sal are pretty tight," I said, stating the obvious.

"Yeah, Sal is pretty amazing. He's like a grandfather to me. He helped me through a lot of stuff. I thought I was over Jasmine's death years ago, but then I had this really bad day at work, which turned into a few bad months. I started seeing Dr. Mike, and then he recommended I start coming to the group therapy sessions. That was about two years ago. I didn't realize some of the crap I had been feeling all of this time later was actually related to old trauma. Mike and Sal both helped me through a tough time. I think I remind Sal of his grandson, and he reminds me of my grandfather. We are meant to be together." Ruben grinned and took another sip of his coffee.

"That's really cool. I'm glad to hear it. I was hesitant to join the group. I was in a pretty dark place after Chris died. Fortunately, my friends and family were there to encourage me to get help."

"That's great. Although you should give yourself some credit too. Admitting that you need help is all you. If you're not ready to get help, then you will just keep moving in place. No one can force you. Family can be persistent as hell, and bug the crap out of you, but you walking through the door is your decision."

I'd never thought about it like that before. I thought about Chris. Maybe he was never fully ready. I'd just pushed and pushed. Ruben was pretty insightful for only being twenty-eight years old.

We finished our breakfast and he walked me back to my car.

"Thanks for breakfast. It was nice not eating alone," Ruben said.

"Anytime. My new roommate is a cat, so that tells you how exciting my social life is."

We laughed and then went our separate ways. On the drive home, I wondered if I had been smiling too much. It felt strange to be talking and laughing with another man. Male colleagues and friends were different because they knew Chris, but Chris had never met Ruben. Yet, I would never have met Ruben, if it wasn't for Chris. My head was spinning.

Beth called just as I was pulling into the driveway. I picked up the phone and told her all about Matilda Chris Josephson.

CHAPTER 13

Tomorrow, June 30, would have been our fifteenth wedding anniversary. Chris and I had started talking a few weeks before his death about where we wanted to celebrate in June. We had always wanted to go back to New York, but we were also thinking something tropical would be fun. A few weeks ago, Beth had offered for her and me go somewhere for the weekend to get out of the house, but I didn't want her paying for me. I had made the decision to try and keep the house, so I was avoiding any large purchases right now. Plus, I had just barely started leaving the house on my own not that long ago, and I wasn't excited about the idea of leaving town yet.

It was Friday night, and I was supposed to be getting ready to meet some of my co-workers for happy hour. I had left work early for a doctor's appointment, but had promised Aubrey, Chantel, and Tess that I would meet them at our favorite happy hour place by 5:30 p.m. It was already five, and I hadn't even changed my clothes. They must have known I was thinking about flaking out again because I started getting texts in a group message telling me I'd better be on my way. I finally compelled myself to get off the couch and go upstairs. I stared at the closet for a few minutes. My eyes kept shifting toward Chris's side, and then I would force myself to look back at mine. I couldn't look at his stuff right now. I needed to pretend I was happy.

I grabbed a pair of black pants and my favorite purple blouse. I reapplied my lipstick and added some blush to my face so I didn't scare anyone. It was almost six by the time I made it to the bar. We all exchanged hugs, and they ordered me a cosmo.

"Finally!" Aubrey said as she moved her empty glass out of the way to make room for mine.

"Yeah, we thought you were standing us up again!" Chantel screeched.

"No, no, I'm here. Sorry, I got caught up with some stuff." I tried to sound cool and collected, not stressed and wound tight.

My cosmo arrived and I started to relax. It was just a night out with some of the girls from work. Aubrey and Chantel were attorneys. Aubrey was married to Jessica, an attorney at a different firm, and they had two kids. Tess, a law clerk, was unhappily engaged. It seemed like she was always telling us about a fight she and Zach had, and then the great makeup sex a few hours later. Chantel was single and loved to flirt. In the four years I'd known her, her longest relationship had lasted about three months. She enjoyed being single and having a good time, so more power to her.

"Let's dance!" Chantel yelled and grabbed my hand.

"I'm okay. I'll meet you guys over there," I said as I reached for my cosmo.

"Okay, girl, you better," Chantel said as she led Aubrey and Tess onto the dance floor. A few minutes passed, and they kept motioning me to join them. I ordered another cosmo. The waiter brought it over and said, "On the house, from that guy." He pointed to a guy wearing a suit, his tie loosened at his neck. Before I could reject the drink, the waiter was off to the next table. I waved at the guy to thank him but was careful not to make eye contact. A minute passed, and then he walked over to my table.

"Hi. I'm Shephard, but my friends call me Shep. You can definitely call me Shep, or whatever you want to call me. Why is such a pretty lady sitting alone here tonight?" He looked me up and down. I felt like I needed to go home, burn these clothes, and take a shower for the next twenty-four hours just to get this guy's scent off of me.

"Hi, I'm Kara. I'm waiting for my husband," I said as I pointed to the wedding ring on my finger.

"Oh, well, that's okay. He's pretty dumb to leave you here all by yourself."

Slimy Shep didn't know the half of it. "Thanks for the drink," I said as I stood up from the table to join my friends on the dance floor. I hadn't danced since my cousin's wedding last fall. Chris and I had a great time. The wedding took place at a winery in Temecula. It was a fun evening of eating, dancing, and celebrating. Chris and I were slow dancing to one of my favorite songs, "(Everything I Do) I Do It for You," by Bryan Adams. He was wearing his navy suit with blue checkered shirt, navy tie, and brown shoes. Chris looked incredibly handsome. I was wearing a flowered blue dress and black heels, and my hair was up. Chris started singing the lyrics in my ear. It was making me giggle, and I was trying to concentrate on not stepping on his feet while we danced.

"Hey, wanna get out of here?" he'd asked and then passionately kissed my lips. I nodded and we were off, saying our quick goodbyes to the wedding party. By the time we made it back to our hotel room, Chris's suit jacket and tie were completely off, his shirt untucked, and my hair was a mess.

I made my escape to the dance floor.

"Hey, who was that guy?" Tess shouted in my ear. I told them the story of Slimy Shep and they all laughed. We danced for another hour and then parted ways.

Sugar was already lying in bed when I arrived home. I changed into some sweats and grabbed one of Chris's T-shirts from the dresser to throw on. I lay in bed, closed my eyes, and thought about that night in Temecula.

I woke up the next morning and dreaded the thought of getting out of bed. Today was anniversary day, but instead of feeling happy and in love, all I felt was sadness. I heaved a big sigh and finally forced myself up. Sugar was already waiting for me downstairs to make her breakfast. I fed her and made myself some coffee. I headed out to the patio. Beth called a few minutes later to confirm we were still on for dinner tonight. I didn't feel like going, but it had been a while since I had been to their house, and I wanted to see everyone.

After my coffee, I grabbed the keys, went into the garage, and sat in Chris's car. His 2004 gray BMW had been sitting in the garage since Mark and Beth had dropped it off a couple of months ago. I remembered after they left that day, I'd sat in the driver's seat and cried for hours. I couldn't stop thinking that this was the last car Chris had driven. I wondered what was going through his mind when he was driving to Pasadena that day. After debating with myself about it for a while, I finally decided to sell the car. It was just sitting in the garage, and I could use the money to pay off a couple of small bills. I was hesitant to get rid of it because we'd had a lot of great memories in that car. Fun times like road trips, singing bad carpool karaoke, and making love in the back seat after that Airborne Toxic Event concert. But seeing the car now just reminded me of the day Chris died. Mark's friend had offered to buy it, so I was going to drop the car off tonight when I went over there for dinner, and they would give me a ride home.

I spent the day doing laundry, looking at photo albums, and thinking about Chris. I took a shower in the late afternoon and got ready to go to Mark and Beth's house. I had been dreading this moment all day. I picked up Chris's keys and stared at the key chain. After a few moments, I removed the keys and put them on the counter. A feeling of uneasiness washed over me. I quickly took a seat at the kitchen table and put the key chain in front of me. I was like a child in a toy store and couldn't help but pick the chain up again. It felt heavy and cool to the touch in my small, unstable hands. Tears flowed again as I continued to hold the key chain and weep into my hands.

I shook my head as I ordered myself to pull it together. I finally summoned the courage to stand up, put the key chain in my pants pocket, grab the car key, and head out to the garage. I hadn't driven the BMW since before Chris's death. I had thought about keeping his car and selling my Mazda3, but mine was a newer, had fewer miles on it, and got better gas mileage.

I held the steering wheel tight as I thought about Chris all the way to my mom's over-fifty-five retirement community apartment. I parked the car and gently rubbed my hands along the steering wheel. "Love you, C," I said softly as I released the wheel and opened the car door. I knew I would be driving it one last time with my mom to Beth's house, but it was the last time I would be alone in it. Saying goodbye to Chris's car was much harder than I had imagined.

I walked through the parking lot and headed to my mom's apartment. It was a nice place and she seemed to enjoy living there. They had lots of activities, so half the time I tried calling her, she was out playing bunco, bingo, or making origami. I loved my mom. She was barely sixty and still had more energy than I did.

I sat in her living room while she finished combing her hair in the bathroom. Mom came out a few minutes later and looked fabulous.

"You ready, Kare?" Mom asked as she was throwing her keys and phone into her purse.

"Mom, do you ever miss Dad?" I asked. I had no idea why that popped out of my mouth. Mom came over and sat next to me on the couch. She put her warm arm around me.

"Of course, Kare. I still think about him a lot. He was the one. I know he wasn't perfect, but you know."

"Yeah, I know." I nodded. "How did you get through it? After Dad died so suddenly of a heart attack at forty, and you had me and Beth. You always made it look so easy."

"Oh, Kare, nothing was easy. You girls were young when Josh died, and my heart was broken. I was so thankful I still had you two. You and Beth actually helped me more than I helped you, I think, even though you didn't know it." Mom patted me on the knee.

"I just miss Chris so much, Mom." I started to cry.

"I know, baby. I know." Mom held me there while I had a complete meltdown on her couch.

"Kare, you'll always miss him. That doesn't go away. Thinking about Chris is the best thing we can do. I still remember the summer beach trips we used to take when you girls were little. We rented that little cottage right on the water. You and Beth playing on the beach, me and your dad sipping wine while we sat on the porch swing, watching and laughing as you girls fought over the sand shovel. Your dad loved you girls very much."

"I know, Mom. We loved him too."

A few minutes later, we cleaned ourselves up and

drove to Mark and Beth's house. We had a fun night playing with Ben and Elijah. Mark barbequed steaks, and we all played Candyland after dinner. After two games, Beth and Mom went to put the boys to bed, and I helped Mark with the dishes.

"How are you really doing, Kare? I know today has to be hard," Mark said as he was washing pans in the sink.

"Yeah, okay. I got out of bed, which is a major accomplishment," I chuckled.

"That's good. Baby steps. We are all very proud of you and are here for you." Mark smiled as he handed me a pan to dry.

"Thanks to you, Beth, Mom, and Dawn. Everyone has been so amazing. I would still be lying in bed today if it wasn't for you guys."

Beth and Mom came downstairs, and we hung out eating cheesecake and drinking coffee. It felt good. Around ten we started to say our goodbyes.

"Thanks again for everything," I said as I hugged Mark and Beth. "Oh, and here are the keys and paperwork." I handed them to Mark, careful not to make eye contact, or I might start to lose it again.

"Thanks, Kare. I'll drop it off at Rick's place tomorrow and bring you the check."

"Let me grab my keys so I can drop you guys off," Beth said as she went into the kitchen.

"Babe, I can take them home," Mark said softly, so as not to wake the twins.

"No, it's okay." Beth kissed Mark on the cheek, and we were out the door. I helped Mom into the passenger front seat of the minivan and then climbed into the back. I looked through the window at Chris's BMW parked on the street where I had left it a few hours ago. The car was all alone, just sitting there in the dark. It probably was wondering where the hell Chris was and what was going on. I was already regretting my decision and angry at myself for selling it. I wiped away a few runaway tears as I turned my head to catch one final glimpse as we drove away.

As the BMW disappeared from my view, I fumbled to find Chris's key chain in my pocket. After a few seconds, I felt the cool steel between my fingers and pulled it out. The touch of the key chain soothed my quick-beating heart. I kept it in my hand until I walked through the front door. Then I sat on the couch and smiled as I added Chris's key chain to mine.

CHAPTER 14

I arrived at the COPE meeting about twenty minutes early because I wanted to catch Jensen before the meeting started. Jensen was talking with Elliot and Jan outside the classroom door. We all said our hellos.

"How was your anniversary last weekend? I was thinking about you," Jan said sweetly.

"It was sad and depressing, but I went over to my sister's house, and that helped. And thank you guys for the text messages. You are always so thoughtful."

"No problem." Elliot smiled.

"Yeah, no problem," Jensen said. "We've all been there. The first year of anniversaries, birthdays, and holidays is the worst." Jensen shook his head.

We chitchatted for a few minutes, and then Mary arrived with some cookies. Elliot and Jan helped her inside to set up. Here was my chance.

"Hey, Jensen, can I ask you a question?"

"Sure, of course."

"After Carlos died, how did you get through it? The loneliness, I mean."

"You mean the not having someone there?" he asked.

"Yeah, just the constant quiet. Not having someone there to talk to about your day. Going to bed alone and waking up alone."

"It sucked. It was the worst. I wasn't in a good place for a while after Carlos died. All of the laughter and inside jokes we shared were all suddenly just gone in an instant. Nights were always the worst. Tossing and turning, waiting for Carlos to walk through the door." Jensen looked at the ground.

"I was so lonely," he said. "I started trying to fill that void anywhere. After about six months of moping around, I started going out again. I wasn't emotionally ready, but I was missing Carlos so much. One night I met this guy at a bar. It was a mix of loneliness and too much alcohol, and I ended up going home with him. He wasn't even my type, really. I just wanted to feel close to someone. A connection again. Big surprise, it was no substitute for Carlos, and after it was all over, the void was there again. I felt so ashamed and guilty."

"I totally get it," I said. "I don't want a relationship, but I just miss the closeness of having someone here. I feel bad even thinking about it. Like I'm cheating on Chris."

"I know you feel like you are cheating, but you're not. You're just lonely, and that's normal. It's okay. We are all human and crave attention and love. That's why you're here. You have us to help."

"I'm so thankful for you guys." I smiled.

"I'm glad you found us." Jensen smiled back. "My advice is you'll know when you're ready. I've been with Andy for about two months now, and things are going pretty well. In the beginning I found myself comparing him to Carlos. The way Andy folded his laundry, ate his pasta, arranged his sock drawer. It was all different from Carlos. I couldn't stop thinking about it. I talked to Mike, and he said it was pretty common to compare our previous spouses to our new lovers. The important thing was not to dwell on it. He said no one will be like Carlos, and that's what made him so special. It will get better, Kara. Friends, family, you guys, Mike—all help fill the hole." Jensen touched his heart.

"Thanks, Jensen." We hugged and then went inside to join the rest of the group.

During the meeting I thought about Slimy Shep. Maybe he would have filled the void, even if just temporarily. Would it have been enough? Would it have been worth it? Some days I would probably have said yes.

A new person joined our group that night. Her name was Shelby, and she reminded me of what I probably looked like when I first started coming to the group. Sad, fatigued, and wondering what the fuck she was doing here. She was attractive, probably in her mid-twenties. During the meeting she introduced herself and said her boyfriend had committed suicide a few weeks ago. They had been together since freshman year of college. After the meeting I caught up with her at the refreshment table. She was a better person than I was—she was actually helping clean up. I remembered my first night I'd barely said anything and had run the hell out of here.

"Hi, Shelby, my name is Kara."

"Hi." She shook my hand.

"I just wanted to say hi and introduce myself." I smiled.

"Thanks. Oh, I wanted to talk to you anyway. I heard from someone you lost your husband earlier this year. I'm sorry." I thought of the word *lost.* Chris wasn't *lost.* I knew exactly where he was. He was dead. His body had been cremated, put in an urn, and was now stored in a cemetery with a plaque saying something about him being a loving husband. I had no idea why that word *lost* irritated me. I knew she was just being nice in phrasing it that way. Why should she be honest and say, "I heard your husband jumped off a building and killed himself?"

"Yeah, thanks." I started to help put the refreshments away.

"Do you think we could chat sometime? I like Mike and the group, but you lost your man too, and it's just been a roller coaster."

"Oh, for sure. Anytime." I gave her my cell phone number. "Jensen, Georgia, and Frank also lost their spouses. I'm sure they would be willing to talk with you too."

"Thanks, I appreciate it." Her eyes started to water. I hugged her.

"It will be okay," I whispered in her ear. I walked

Shelby to her car, and she promised to text me when she made it home.

I started walking toward my own car when I heard a familiar voice. I looked a few cars over and saw Mike on his cell phone.

"Okay, okay, yes, I understand. I gotta go." And then he abruptly hung up.

"Hey, Kara," Mike said as he walked over. Shoot, he'd seen me. I hoped he didn't think I was eavesdropping.

"Hey, Mike. Sorry, I was just saying goodbye to Shelby."

"Oh no, I saw. That was really nice. I'm really glad you guys connected." So, Mike had been creepily watching us. I laughed to myself.

"Is everything okay?" I asked.

"Oh, yeah. It was just my ex-wife. Trying to figure out our daughter's birthday."

"Wow, nice. I didn't know you had a daughter."

"Yes, Hannah is twelve, and I have a son, Liam, nine. It's hard with the custody stuff. I have them on odd years for their birthdays, so she gets them this year, but trying to plan a time for me to drop off my gift for Hannah is apparently impossible."

"Oh no, I'm sorry."

"No, no. I'm fine. I'll let you go. Be safe driving home," Mike said as he started walking away. I felt so bad. Mike was always there for us, listening to our crap all of the time. I always assumed he had a great job, enjoyed helping others, and had a perfect family life.

"Do you want to get some coffee or something?" I asked.

He turned around. "Sure, that sounds good."

We walked over to Rosie's and each ordered coffee.

"So, what's going on with you?" he asked. "Work seems to be plugging along, and you're getting back into routine."

"Yeah, it's falling back into place." I told him about selling Chris's car. I also told him all about Sugar and how she had been a great roommate these past few months.

"Pets are the best. They love us unconditionally." Mike smiled.

"Yeah, and they don't talk back," I said. We laughed.

"How long have you been divorced?" I asked. I wasn't sure if it was an appropriate question to ask, but I wanted to know.

"Well, we separated about two years ago, and then we finally signed the divorce papers last year. Definitely some of the hardest years of my life. My poor kids. We try and not let them hear us argue, but they know. They're smart."

"Yeah, I heard divorce is like a death in the family. Sorry, I know, bad joke." I smiled.

"No, you're right, in a way. You know, when you get married, you imagine yourself being with this person for the rest of your life. You guys growing old together. Then life happens, and you start not liking each other very much anymore. She complains I work too much, and then I complain all she does is spend our money. And so on. It just breaks down from there."

"You always seem so put together. You're allowed to be human too, you know."

"Yeah, I know. I psychoanalyze myself all of the time. I drive myself crazy." Mike chuckled.

"I promise I won't tell anyone you're human."

"Okay, good. I wouldn't want to ruin my image."

My cell phone went off, notifying me I had a text. I quickly read Shelby's text saying she'd made it home, and I texted her back a smiley face emoji.

"Shelby just texted to let me know she made it home safe."

"That's nice. I'm glad she reached out to you."

"Yeah, I hope I can help her. I definitely don't feel like a role model."

"Don't sell yourself short. You have come a long way these past months. Losing someone suddenly is a shock. The depth of the loss is felt differently. For example, a sister losing her brother is different than a husband losing his wife. Both relationships are special and important, but each loss is grieved in different ways."

"Yeah, it makes sense."

"I'm glad she's reaching out to you. You know how it feels to lose your life partner. And now to put the pieces of your life back together. You're a strong person."

"Thanks. I definitely couldn't have done it without my family, friends, you, and the group."

We finished our coffee and walked back to our cars.

"Thanks, Kara. It was nice chatting."

"Anytime. I'll send you my bill." We both laughed and said our goodbyes. I drove home feeling happy. It had felt nice to connect with Mike. I think we all forgot he was a real person with problems, like us.

I got home and plopped on the couch next to Sugar. "Hi, sweet girl," I said. Sugar nuzzled my arm. "I think I need to go see your daddy."

The following Saturday I fulfilled my promise and went to Chris's gravesite. I hadn't been there since the plaque was put on the wall. I brought flowers and carefully arranged them in the plastic floral vase. I stared at the plaque that masked his ashes.

Christopher Thomas McKay
Loving Husband, Son, Brother & Uncle
May He Rest in Peace
January 7, 1980 – January 25, 2018

It was always weird to see Chris's actual name, Christopher. I had never heard him called Christopher, except by a friend in college who called him Christopher Robin as a joke, but the nickname had stuck throughout college. Wow, I hadn't thought about that in years. I wondered what had ever happened to that guy, Richard. He was called Big R.

My mind was wandering. I placed my hand gently on the plaque for a moment.

"Hey, C. This is a nice place. Quiet. You would have liked it." I looked around. Large trees, green grass, and benches carefully placed and maintained to help us survivors grieve. I kneeled down and tried to keep my fidgeting to a minimum. I was getting anxious about what I needed to tell Chris. I finally blurted it out.

"I was thinking. I've been mad at you for leaving me alone, but I recently realized it's more than that. I'm also mad you took away our future. We promised to be together forever. You promised me. Our wedding vows. You broke those. We were supposed to grow old and ugly together. Now you'll be remembered as a reasonably young, handsome guy, and I'll be the one to die ugly, old, and alone." I chuckled to myself.

"So, I finally spoke to Dr. Barnes a few weeks ago. John had told him about you, about what happened, the day after, and Dr. Barnes called the house that day. Beth spoke with him. I didn't because I could barely get out of bed. It was probably better because I wanted to yell at him. I wanted to tell him he was a bad doctor who'd killed you, and maybe if he had been a better doctor, you would still be alive. I blamed him for a long time. I blamed everyone, especially you. I even blamed myself for being such an ignorant and stupid wife, but Mike and the group have helped me get over some of that anger. Instead of yelling at Dr. Barnes, I explained to him that you killed a part of me too. My insides were worn out, and I'd been living like a ghost since you left me. Dr. Barnes was very sorry and felt horrible that he wasn't able to keep you 'under control.' I don't think you were ever fully controlled, were you? The therapy and the meds were ways to try and tame you, but I know now they were just muting you. And putting you on mute was like putting a Band-Aid on a gunshot wound. That was my fault, and I apologize. I'm sorry if I made you feel like you had to shut yourself up in order to be better for me, to make our marriage work. I pressured you to take your meds and to be a certain way, and for what? You were miserable. No, not all of the time, I know. I see that now. There was nothing wrong with you. It's the goddamn system. We treat mental health like it's contagious and don't want to acknowledge it for what it is—a fucking life-long disease. There is no magic cure for depression or bipolar disorder. And, in the words of Dr. Barnes, sometimes it can't be 'controlled.' I wish you had let me in, Chris. I wish you had let me see the real you. I also wish I *wanted* to see the real you, that I had been more understanding when you were having trouble adjusting to the medications, or unraveling from the side effects, or just having a bad fucking day. You were never alone, and I feel like shit thinking you felt that way."

I couldn't hold the tears in any longer. The tears came, but I powered through them. I had waited too long to come here and say these things to Chris. It was time. "I sold the BMW. I didn't want to, but I couldn't look at it. It reminded me of you too much. I know that sounds stupid because I want to keep the house, which has you all over it. I wear your old T-shirts to bed, trying to inhale the last bit of your scent. I haven't washed them yet because I don't want to lose the feel of you on them. I still can't really look at your side of the closet, and I hid your wedding ring in the nightstand. I've been trying to gain the nerve to work on these things, but I don't know what I'm supposed to do. I just miss you so damn much. You're all I think about. I've gone back to work, trying to get into routine. Beth told me she is going to sign me up for cooking glasses…yeah, I thought you would think that's funny."

I spoke to Chris for another hour, just babbling on. It felt good to talk to him and get these thoughts and feelings out in the open. I knew he probably couldn't hear me, but part of me felt like he did.

CHAPTER 15

It had been 273 days since Chris's death. He'd missed our anniversary in June and my birthday in September a few weeks ago. My co-workers had celebrated with lunch and a birthday cake for me, and my family took me out to dinner and gave me a gift card for a spa day. It was a great birthday by normal standards, except Chris wasn't there. It was strange celebrating without him. I kept looking for him and then realized he wasn't coming this year. He would never celebrate another birthday again.

Now another month had gone by, and nothing had changed. I fed Sugar, grabbed a bottle of wine, and went into Chris's office. I snickered at the damaged furniture and picture frames. I wasn't too concerned about replacing any of that stuff. I sat in his comfy office chair and started thinking about the upcoming holidays. He'd loved watching movies and giving out candy on Halloween. We would try and hit at least one haunted house, hayride, or corn maze during the month of

October. We always had a blast. I thought about Claudia and her missing her dad on Halloween too. Thanksgiving was always a fun holiday as well, but it was also a lot of work. Fortunately, we switched off hosting and did potluck style to help out whomever was hosting. Chris's parents normally went skiing Thanksgiving week, so we didn't share that holiday with them. We tried to make it to Santa Barbara every other year or two to spend Thanksgiving with John. Celine came from a large family in the central coast and Bay Area, so they had a big party for the holidays. It was always a lot of fun. I remembered a few years ago years ago we'd driven to Santa Barbara for Thanksgiving and were staying the weekend with John and Celine. They had a beautiful home on the water. John was a pediatrician, and Celine was an interior home designer. She didn't have to work—she came from money, and John made a very good salary—but she was naturally very good at her job. She made it look easy. I remembered it was Thanksgiving evening, and I was helping Celine and John clean up the kitchen. Isabella had gone to bed a few hours earlier, but Noah was wide awake. Chris volunteered to read Noah a bedtime story. John had laughed and told Chris, "I hope you know what you're getting yourself into."

After we finally finished the endless sea of dishes, we noticed it had been really quiet upstairs.

"Either Noah killed Chris, or they both fell asleep," John said as we all walked up the stairs to Noah's room.

The door was half open and we all peered inside. Chris was sleeping on the bed, snoring, mouth completely open, with a book in his left hand. Noah was playing quietly on the floor with some toys.

We all started to laugh. Noah yelled really loud, "What, what is it?"

Chris was startled awake. "What? What happened?" he asked as he wiped his hand across his mouth.

"Thanks, Noah, for putting your uncle to sleep," John said as he picked Noah up and put him in his bed.

"Hey, that's a good bedtime story. You try staying awake reading it after a gigantic Thanksgiving dinner," Chris said as he patted his stomach.

"Don't feel bad, Chris. John falls asleep pretty much every night reading the same book to Noah," Celine chuckled.

"The book is cursed," John laughed as he grabbed it off the floor.

"What, Daddy? What's cursed?" Noah asked sweetly.

"Ah, nothing. Let's try this again," John said as he lay in bed with Noah and started to read the story.

"I'll meet you guys in a few minutes," John whispered.

"I doubt that," Chris said as he shut the door.

"I'm going to go check on Isabella," Celine said. "I'll be down in a few. Feel free to open another bottle of wine." She walked toward Isabella's room.

Chris and I made our way back to the kitchen. I was stuffed with food but found myself still eating sweets that had been left on the counter.

"Oh my God. Why am I eating this? I'm so full but can't stop myself," I said as I wiped chocolate brownie crumbs from my face.

"You can't control yourself. It's a sickness. I don't know what I'm going to do with you." Chris laughed as he came up behind me and gave me a kiss on the cheek. He started scanning the wine bottles left on the counter and opened one. He poured us each a glass, and we went outside on the patio. It was cold, but the air felt crisp and welcoming.

About twenty minutes later, John and Celine came downstairs. They each poured themselves a glass of wine and joined us outside.

"Finally, woke up, hmm?" Chris asked, motioning toward John.

"Yeah, I started dozing off again. That damn book is a cure for insomniacs everywhere," John chuckled.

"You guys are just getting old and don't have the stamina anymore," I said. Celine and I looked at each other and laughed.

"What? Oh, I have stamina. I have it coming out of my ears," John said as he took another sip of wine.

"Yeah, I have so much stamina, you can't even comprehend the amount of stamina I have," Chris said as he winked at me.

"So, pushing Noah out of his bed so you could sleep, what was that?" I asked innocently.

"A power nap. All people with great stamina take power naps. Our bodies are extremely efficient, we don't need a full night's sleep. We rely only on short bouts of rest to replenish our energy," Chris said.

John nodded in agreement.

"Five bucks says you both are asleep within two seconds of hitting the pillow tonight," Celine said.

"You're on," Chris and John said simultaneously. We later compared notes, and Celine won the five dollars from both Chris and John, though they were adamant they were just taking power naps, so that shouldn't count.

Chris was slow to get out of bed the next morning. He had drunk too much yesterday, and I called him out on it.

"C, you shouldn't technically be drinking at all with your medication," I said gently as I sat in bed fully dressed, waiting for him to get up.

"I'm taking the meds, okay? I hate taking the fucking meds, but I do it for you. The least I can do is have a drink or two once in a while. Jesus Christ, get off my back!" Chris readjusted himself in bed.

"I know, I know. I just worry about you. I'm glad you're taking your stuff and doing well. I just want you to be careful. And it was much more than two drinks, but…" I decided to stop talking. I didn't want to fight, but I also didn't want Chris mixing too much alcohol with his meds. I was a realist, and I was okay with him having a drink here and there, but he seemed to be doing it more often lately. Chris and I had had many conversations about us both completely giving up alcohol. It would be hard, but we could do it together. He didn't want me to, though. He said it would make him feel even worse knowing I couldn't relax with a bottle of wine in our own home if I wanted to. Now I look back and realize I should have just thrown out all of the damn alcohol in the house. Maybe it would have made a difference.

"Whatever. I'm going to take a shower." Chris stood up, grabbed some clothes, and headed down the hall to the restroom.

I went downstairs to meet up with the family. I knew they had probably already been up for a while. I found John at the kitchen table.

"Hi. Sorry, we slept in a bit."

"Ah, must be nice." John smirked. "I'm just jealous. Isabella and Noah have no concept of sleeping in." He yawned as he reached for his cup of coffee.

"Where are the kids and Celine?" I asked.

"She took them over to her parents for a little bit. I think she and her sisters were going to do some early Black Friday shopping. God help them."

"Right." I smiled.

"Hey, on another subject. How's Chris doing? He seems good. Happy," John said.

"Yeah, he seems to be doing pretty good for the most part. He is taking his meds, working."

"He shouldn't be drinking while he is on the medication, though," John said sternly.

"I know. He knows. He was just having fun last night."

"Maybe I should mention it to him?" John asked.

"I said something this morning, and he bit my head off, so I wouldn't suggest it."

"Seriously?"

"You know Chris. He knows he shouldn't be, and it made him a little sick this morning. He just gets frustrated."

"I know. It sucks."

Chris came down a few minutes later. He looked better and refreshed after his shower. I thought about telling John about Chris's drinking lately, but I didn't want to ruin the weekend. Chris was having a great time, and he knew what he was doing. He knew he needed to stop the drinking. I noticed Chris didn't have anything else to drink the rest of the weekend.

About a month later, Chris and I went to my work holiday party. It was always a nicely catered, open-bar party after hours at the office. Everyone dressed up and we had a good time. We were well into the evening, and Chris and I were talking with an attorney in my firm, Todd, and his girlfriend, Molly. Todd and I used to work closely together, but Todd had made partner recently, and management had made some staff reassignments. He was always nice and appreciative of staff. Molly worked from home as a financial planner. We were talking about Chris's new book. I stepped away for a minute to refill my drink, and by the time I came back, I could tell things had gone south.

"Glad to hear you're feeling better. I know that's pretty scary," Todd said. "My sister has depression, and she can't leave the house sometimes."

"Although some days we think she is just faking it because she doesn't want to go to work," Molly chimed in.

I looked at Chris. The expression on his face was of complete shock.

"Yeah, you know us mentally ill people, we try and get out of going to work all of the time," Chris said sarcastically as put his drink down and walked out of the office. I was trying to catch up to him. Damn these short legs. I finally caught up to him at the elevator.

"What the fuck? You tell our personal life stories to some asshole named Todd? I'm glad you and your co-worker buddies can have a good laugh at my expense." Chris was pissed, and I didn't blame him. The elevators doors opened and I followed him in. Luckily, no one else was on the elevator.

"I'm sorry, C. I told Todd in confidence once. It was after you and I had a fight, and I was really upset."

"You shouldn't be telling anyone about me. About us. I don't need them staring at me, waiting to explode, or pitying you for being married to someone like me. Oh, poor Kara, married to the fucking nutjob."

"It's not like that. I love you. I'm sorry. I didn't think Todd would tell anyone else. He has been drinking tonight, so maybe that's why he said it. I don't fucking know what his problem is."

"Glad you are making excuses for him. You are unbelievable."

We finally made it to the car. "Give me the keys," Chris demanded.

"No, I'm driving. You're too angry to drive."

"Give me the fucking keys, Kare. I'm fine."

"No, not till you calm down."

"Fuck this!" Chris started walking away.

"Where the fuck are you going?" I yelled.

"I'll fucking walk. I don't want to see you right now anyway."

I jumped in the driver's seat and started bawling. I'd

only had one glass of wine but had a throbbing headache already.

"Fuck!" I hit the steering wheel with my fists.

I calmed down after a few minutes and drove home. The house was still dark when I pulled into the driveway. I went inside, and there was no sign of Chris. I went into the bathroom where he kept his meds. I was looking at the refill dates and counting the number of pills in each of the bottles.

"You fucking asshole, I knew it!" I yelled to myself.

Chris walked through the front door a little after 2:00 a.m. I got up from the couch and met him in the kitchen. I could smell the alcohol on him from across the room.

"You fucking asshole. You stopped taking your meds. That's why you haven't been getting as sick when you drink lately."

"Why the fuck are you going through my stuff? You are the asshole here, telling your whole goddamn office about me. You guys have nothing else better to do than talk about me? You guys are pathetic."

"Don't change the subject. You haven't been taking your prescriptions. How long has it been? Since Thanksgiving? Before?"

"I don't know. It doesn't matter. I know what I'm doing."

"Obviously. You are the fucking perfect picture of health."

"Goddamn it, Kara. I won't die if I go off my meds for a few weeks. The fucking world will not end."

"It might. You need your meds. I don't know what the fuck you will do if you aren't on them."

"What, do you think I'll hurt you? Hurt someone else?"

"No, I think you'll hurt yourself or God only knows what."

"The meds make me a zombie. I hate feeling like I'm not in control of my own body. Plus, I can't sleep, or some pills make me so tired it's hard to get out of bed. I don't know if I'm fucking coming or going half the time."

"We should talk to Dr. Barnes then. We can figure out a new dosage or something."

"I'm tired of it. I'm fucking tired of the pills, Dr. Barnes, the fucking talking about my feelings. It's fucking exhausting, and I'm done."

"C, don't say that. We can get through this."

"I'm going to bed." Chris walked out of the room and went to the guest room.

I was so angry. I was mad at Todd for being a jerk. I was mad at myself for ever telling Todd in a moment of weakness that Chris and I were struggling because Chris was once again trying a new medication that fucked with his moods. And I was mad at Chris for stopping his meds and not telling anyone. He knew better. Or, at least, I thought he knew better. Apparently, I was wrong again.

I tossed and turned in our bed for the next few hours and then got out of bed when the sun came up. I went outside to the patio and called John. I told him everything.

"Jesus Christ, Kare. Why didn't you tell me this sooner?"

"I know. I'm sorry. I thought it was under control. I thought he could control it."

"And if I ever meet that fucking Todd guy…"

"I know, I know. Trust me."

"Okay, I'll call Chris in a few hours and feel it out. I'll come down if I need to. Stupid ass, getting off of his meds. He knows better."

"I know. Thanks, John."

Chris came out to the kitchen around noon. He still looked tired.

"Hey, can I make you something to eat?" I asked softly.

"No, thanks. Just coffee." He walked over to the coffee pot and filled his cup to the brim.

"I'm sorry, C. I shouldn't have told that stupid Todd guy anything about us." I sat down at the kitchen table while Chris stood at the counter.

"I know. I get it. I know I'm not the easiest person to live with, and sometimes you need to talk to someone. Just don't talk to that asshole."

"Agreed."

"I'm sorry about the meds. I just needed a break. All of the side effects and bullshit that comes along with taking them are so frustrating. Knowing that this is something I'm not just going to grow out of anymore is mind numbing. This is me. This is my life. I just need to accept it."

"Chris, we have each other. We can do anything together."

"Kare, I love you, and I appreciate that. I wouldn't be here without you. It's just hard because you can never fully understand what I'm talking about. What I'm feeling. I try to express it, but it never comes out right. Sometimes there are just no words. Sometimes alcohol is the best way to numb myself for a few hours and not worry about anything. I'm able to forget for a little while and believe I'm just a regular asshole like everyone else."

"I know." I got up and hugged Chris. It felt good to have him in my arms again. "I know, C."

John called Chris that afternoon and they were on the phone for over an hour.

Chris walked into the living room after he hung up with John.

"You told on me?" Chris shook his head.

"Well, you left me no choice."

"Big Daddy John was mad," Chris said.

"He loves you," I said.

"I know."

"Now what?" I asked.

"I'll call Dr. Barnes on Monday and see what the next step is."

"Thanks, C. I love you."

"Love you too."

Chris called Dr. Barnes and was back on track within the next few weeks. The Monday after the holiday party, I went to Todd's office.

"Hey, how was your weekend?" Todd asked as he put down the brief he was reading and motioned for me to take a seat across from his desk.

"Okay. Hey…" I started to say.

"Hey, before you say anything, I'm sorry if Molly or I offended Chris. We didn't mean to say anything out of turn."

"No, I know. It's just a sensitive subject, and I thought our conversation had been private."

"It was."

"Well, you told Molly."

"Yeah, sorry. I think we were talking about her sister, and then I mentioned Chris. I didn't mean any harm."

"I get it. If we can just keep personal stuff between us, that would be great."

"Yeah, of course. Again, I'm sorry. I don't want this to affect our friendship." Todd stood up and walked around the desk to where I was sitting. He leaned back on his desk and said, "You know, if you ever need anything, you can always come to me. My door is always open."

"Thanks, I appreciate that." I started to feel a little uncomfortable, so I stood up.

"Kara, you're a beautiful woman. You deserve a guy that can treat you right. A real man," Todd said as he gently touched my unwelcoming arm.

"I gotta go." I yanked my arm back and ran out of his office. What the hell had just happened? I felt like I was in one of those Lifetime movies that never end well. Maybe I was totally misinterpreting Todd's sympathy as him hitting on me. I replayed it in my head the rest of the day. One thing I did know for sure was I would never let Chris know what happened. He already hated Todd and now had even more reason to.

After Chris's death, Todd texted me that he was sorry. I was glad he didn't show up to the funeral. I probably would have yelled at him for being such a jerk to Chris and caused a huge scene.

A few weeks after I returned to work, I was there late one night, and Todd came by my desk.

"Hey, Kara. Working late?"

"Yeah, just trying to finish this last piece for Syd's ex parte we want to try and file tomorrow."

"I'll be done in an hour. Do you want to grab dinner?" Todd asked.

I smiled. "Todd, I'd rather eat shit and die than eat with you." I turned my chair around and started typing again. I heard him walk back toward his office. I smiled at the picture of Chris sitting on my desk. It was the picture of us when we had gone to Catalina for our eighth wedding anniversary. Chris had taken the picture, and we were both smiling, with the ocean as a backdrop. It was one of my favorite photos of us.

CHAPTER 16

It was the first Saturday in November. Sal and Irene were celebrating their fiftieth wedding anniversary and had invited all of the group to the party. They had rented out a hall in Newport Beach to celebrate. Some of the group were getting hotel rooms to avoid the drive home. I wasn't going to get a room until Shelby asked if we could share one. I thought it would be nice to have someone to carpool with and a date to the party. I hadn't dressed up for anything like this in a long time. I decided to wear my emerald-green wrap dress. It was comfortable but elegant at the same time. Shelby and I helped each other put on makeup and fix our hair in our hotel room.

"Feels like I'm getting ready for the prom," Shelby laughed as she sprayed some perfume.

I looked in the mirror. I thought about Chris and how he would have been teasing me to hurry up by now.

"Fifty years. That is so awesome," I said.

"Yeah, that is pretty cool. I'm sad Jared and I will never have that," Shelby said as she slipped on her heels.

"I know, I was totally thinking about that with me and Chris. We had talked about renewing our wedding vows on our twentieth wedding anniversary. It was going to be a ceremony right on the beach. Just small, with close friends and family, you know." I looked away from the mirror.

"Kara, stop. We're not here to be sad tonight. We promised we're taking the night off from being sad. Jared and Chris are just out of town, and we are going to have a girls' night out, okay? Remember?"

"I know, I know. I promised."

We grabbed our purses and coats and were on our way. The hall was beautifully decorated with bouquets of flowers, candles, and photos of Sal, Irene, and their family. As you walked in the room, there was a gigantic photo of Sal and Irene from their wedding day. Sal looked so handsome in his tux, and Irene was gorgeous in her beautiful gown. Luckily, there were no seat assignments, so we could sit wherever. People already had drinks in their hands and were mingling around the room. Shelby and I dropped our bags and coats at a table and went to the bar. We each ordered a cosmo. I saw Jan and Elliot chatting with Claudia in the corner. I waved hello, and Shelby and I walked over.

"Hey, you guys. You all look great!" Jan said as she came in for hugs.

"You too," I said. Jan looked like a completely different person with a dress and makeup on. "Is Lynn here?"

"No, she wasn't feeling well."

"Aw, sorry to hear that," I said.

"This is such a beautiful place," Claudia said as she looked around the room.

"It's amazing," I said.

Sal came by and introduced us to his family, Irene, Abraham, and Rachel. Others had met them before, but it was my first time. They were all so kind and funny, like Sal. I couldn't help but think about Jacob and how much they all missed him. Irene looked stunning. I hoped I look that good when I was seventy. Hell, I wanted to look that good now.

We were all herded to our seats soon after the introductions. We heard beautiful speeches from Abraham and a family friend, Ezra, who had been in their wedding fifty years ago. Sal then stood up to make his own speech.

"Irene, I love you. Thank you for putting up with me for these fifty years. I know it's hard living with a stud like myself, but you've been a real doll." Everyone laughed.

"No, now I'm being serious for a minute. This lady is incredible. All kidding aside, I love you so much, and I can't imagine not being with you every day. I look forward to waking up in the morning just to see your face. You are my everything, and I thank you." Irene was crying and went up and kissed Sal.

"Thanks, everyone! Enjoy! Love you all!" Sal said as he handed the microphone back to the DJ.

Sal escorted Irene to the dance floor. Frank Sinatra's

"The Best Is Yet to Come" filled the room. Shelby patted my back and headed toward the bar. Sal and Irene were so adorable. Chris had loved Frank Sinatra. Our favorite Sinatra song to dance to was "The Way You Look Tonight." I thought about us slow dancing on our patio. My head on Chris's chest, Chris nuzzling my hair. I looked over at Shelby. She was talking and laughing with some guy by the bar. I worried about her. There was no doubt that she had loved Jared, but she seemed like one of those people that couldn't be without someone for too long. Constantly searching for love, someone to share her bed with. I understood the loneliness. Like Jensen said, it sucked.

Kara, I told myself, enough of the pity party. I'm going to freshen up, come back, and have another drink.

As I exited the restroom, I ran into Sal.

"Beautiful speech, Sal. Truly sweet."

"Thanks, kid. I was thinking about you and Chris tonight."

"You were?" I asked, wondering why thoughts of us would creep in and ruin a beautiful evening.

"I was thinking it's not fair that you and Chris will not be celebrating your fiftieth. It breaks my heart. But I was also thinking, it's time to move on, my dear. I want you to experience a fiftieth wedding anniversary with someone. Just because Chris isn't here, doesn't mean you can't find love again."

"Sal, it's not that simple."

"You complicate things, kid. You deserve to find love

again. You're young. Don't shut yourself off from the world. From happiness."

An older guy with a fedora came by and patted Sal on the back. "Hey, Sal. Tell Jimmy about your fishing trip last summer."

"Think about it," Sal told me. He kissed me on the cheek and then started to tell the group about his fishing trip last year.

I thought about what Sal had said the rest of the night. I saw Jensen and met his boyfriend, Andy. They seemed really happy together, laughing and dancing. Was Sal right? Could I love again? He didn't understand. He still had his wife. I didn't need love because I'd already had it. I just wanted a distraction to fill the loneliness. I stopped at the bar and ordered a rum and Coke. I went outside to hear myself think. On my way out, I saw Mike and a woman talking.

"Hi, Kara," he said.

"Hi, Mike."

"This is my girlfriend, Veronica."

"Hi, nice to meet you," she said. She held her hand out for me to shake it. It took me a second to realize what she was doing. I shook her hand. Veronica was very pretty and I felt like such an idiot. Why had I thought Mike needed me to talk to when he had a beautiful girlfriend probably waiting for him at home that night?

We chatted for another minute, and then I finally made it outside. I looked over and saw Ruben holding a beer bottle and staring into the darkness. It was quiet except for faint music from the hall in the background.

I wasn't sure if I should say anything. I changed directions and started walking the other way.

"Hey, Kara." Dang, he'd seen me. I was always getting caught. I turned around and started walking toward him.

"Hey, Ruben."

He was wearing a dark gray suit, blue shirt, and gray striped tie. His hair was disheveled, and he looked like he hadn't slept in a week.

"Are you okay?" I asked.

"Yeah, yeah. Just tired."

"We missed you in group last week."

"It's been a rough couple of weeks."

"I'm sorry. Is it your mom? Is she okay?"

"No, no, she's still doing well, thanks. My girlfriend and I broke up."

"Oh, no. I'm sorry."

"Yeah, I found out she was cheating on me, and I ended it. She was cheating on me with her old boyfriend. How fucking cliché."

"She sucks," I said, trying to make Ruben laugh. He cracked a smile.

"Nothing an open bar can't fix," Ruben said as he finished off his beer. "Do you want another?"

"Sure, I'll come with you. I need to check on Shelby anyway."

We walked in, and I saw Shelby at our table, grabbing her coat and purse. I walked over.

"Hey, I was looking for you. I'm taking off," Shelby said.

"Taking off? Where?"

"Dave—this guy Dave is really nice, and we are going to hang out at his hotel room."

"Dave? Really?"

"Yeah, don't worry. He's harmless." She pointed toward a bald guy talking to Sal.

"Hey, don't do this. You're not thinking straight."

"Oh my God. You're not my mother, Kara."

"I know, I just want to make sure you're not going to do something you'll regret."

"Regret? I'm a grown-ass woman. I can do whatever the fuck I want. Maybe you'd feel better if you got laid yourself."

I held up my hands. "Okay, okay. I'm not going to get into this with you right now. Just call me if you need anything."

"I'm taking my car."

"What? How am I supposed to get back to the hotel?"

"Get a ride. Call an Uber."

I was pissed. By this time Ruben had come by the table with my rum and Coke.

"Hey, Shelby," he said.

"Hey, Ruben," she said as she stormed off.

"Wow, what was that?" Ruben asked. We sat down and I told him.

"I kind of thought she was a little high maintenance," Ruben said as he shook his head. "I can give you a ride, no problem."

It was almost ten o'clock, and the dancing and fun were still going strong.

"Hey, do you want to dance?" Ruben shouted.

"What?" I knew what he had asked, but I wanted to give myself a moment to figure out what I was going to say.

He repeated the question.

"Um, I'm not that good of a dancer. No, thanks."

"Come on," Ruben said as he stood up and grabbed my hand.

We headed toward the dance floor. Justin Timberlake's "Can't Stop the Feeling" was playing. We joined Jensen, Andy, Elliot, Jan, and Claudia on the dance floor. I saw Efrain talking with Sal and Mike near the bar. Monique and her husband, Sean, and Mary and her fiancé, Lucas, joined us on the dance floor. It was funny, this group of ours. All of us had lived in different worlds until we each suffered the tragic loss of a loved one. Their deaths were the bond that we all shared now. If our dead spouses, mothers, fathers, daughters, sons, friends, could see us now, dancing and making jokes through our grief.

By midnight, the servers were cleaning up, and all of us were saying our goodbyes. Ruben had stopped drinking a couple of hours ago so was able to drive me back to the hotel. Fortunately, I had remembered to get the keycard from Shelby before she ditched me. I was feeling pretty buzzed and just wanted to crawl into bed, close my eyes, and dream about Chris, but Sal's words kept interrupting my thoughts.

I tossed and turned until I heard Shelby knocking on the door around eight the next morning. She was pretty hung over, and I was still pissed, so the car ride home was extremely quiet.

I never saw Shelby again after that day. After a few days of being mad, I had decided to check on her. Maybe she was right, and I was being too judgmental. I called and left a voicemail and texted her that I was sorry we'd fought and said I wanted to talk. She texted me back and said she was fine. Mike also tried to get in contact with her, but she didn't respond to him. I often thought about her and hoped she was okay.

CHAPTER 17

My mom, Beth, and Dawn had come over Saturday night. I wanted to make a special dinner to thank them for all that they had done for me over the last ten months. I wasn't much of a cook but wanted to show my appreciation somehow. I had learned how to make lasagna in my new cooking class. It was an easy-to-follow recipe, and it made a ton of leftovers, which was great. As we sat down to the table to eat, I started with a quick toast.

"To my best friend and my family. Thank you for everything. I love you all so much." We all raised our glasses and toasted, then started to eat.

"Wow, this is delicious, Kare," Dawn said.

"Why do you sound surprised?" I asked lovingly.

"Um, I remember the chicken pot pie incident." Dawn smiled.

"Wait, what is this chicken pot pie incident?" Beth asked.

"Is it similar to the green bean casserole incident Thanksgiving 2004?" Mom asked.

"You guys are all so hilarious. And yes, all of it." I laughed. I thought about the time I was going to surprise Chris with a roast dinner. He had been gone at a conference for a few days and was coming home late Friday night. I went grocery shopping Thursday night after work to buy all of the ingredients. I woke up extra early Friday morning so I had time to put everything together before work. I followed the recipe exactly, double-checking the steps as I went along. I thought about the roast all day at work. I was so excited to come home and smell that wonderful dinner-in-the-Crock-Pot smell. Well, I came home and didn't smell anything. That's weird, I thought. I threw all of my stuff on the couch and ran to the kitchen. Apparently, I had turned the Crock-Pot to warm rather than low. I was so furious at myself. What a moron!

Chris had come downstairs shortly after my grim discovery.

"Hey, I didn't know you were home," I said as I walked over to him, and we kissed.

"Gary dropped me off a few minutes ago," Chris said as he walked over to the Crock-Pot. "Dinner?" he asked innocently.

"It was supposed to be," I said as I made a sad face.

"It's the thought that counts. You're the best." Chris came over and gave me a big hug.

"I feel like such an idiot. I wanted dinner to be perfect," I whined.

"It is. You're here, right? I'm here. That is perfection at its best." Chris kissed me and then grabbed his cell. "And pizza is perfection too." He laughed as he dialed the number to our favorite pizza place.

I told Mom, Beth, and Dawn the story, and they were crying tears of laughter.

"We love you, Kare, just the way you are," Beth said, laughing uncontrollably.

During dessert I wanted to share my news. I let them take the first few bites of the butterscotch brownies before I told them I wanted to go to the Turner Building. Mom finally broke the awkward silence.

"What did Dr. Mike say?"

"I haven't told Dr. Mike."

"Maybe you should talk to him first and see what he says," Dawn interjected.

"I don't need to tell Mike everything I do," I said defensively.

"That's true. You're an adult. We just worry about you because we love you," Beth said.

"I know. I'll think about talking to Mike about it. I promise."

"Awesome. Let's open up another bottle of wine and another bottle of grape juice for our breast-pumping friend," Beth said lovingly.

"I hate you guys." Dawn laughed as she took another swig of her grape juice.

I did end up talking to Mike about going to the scene of where it had all happened. Where it had all ended. He was very supportive and said he would go with me if I wanted. Mike also suggested I talk to some of the group members before I decided. Some of them had done the same thing and would be able to give me different perspectives.

A few minutes before our next meeting started, I caught Sal at the food table grabbing some cookies before the meeting.

"Hi, Sal, how are you tonight?"

"Still breathing, so I guess that's a good sign. For me anyway. Maybe not for my wife," he chuckled. "How are you sweetheart? You doing okay?"

"Yes, thanks. One day at a time. I was talking to Mike and told him I was thinking of going to the Turner Building, where, you know, Chris, um, where it happened. Mike suggested I talk with some of the group members before deciding to go or not." I stumbled over my words.

"Oh. Yes, I know a few people you can speak with. Are you free after the meeting? I'll see if I can gather a few of us together."

"Sure, that would be great, thanks," I said as I made my way to a seat.

After the meeting Sal, Efrain, Claudia, and I walked across the street to Rosie's Cafe to get some coffee. We sat in a large booth in the corner. All of us ordered coffee except Sal, who opted for a milkshake.

"Thanks for taking the time to meet. I really appreciate it," I said as I poured some milk into my coffee cup.

"No problem. We're always here if you need us," Efrain said as he looked around the table.

"I told everyone that you were thinking about going to the Turner Building to see where Chris died," Sal said. "Efrain and Claudia have some input they can share with you. Who wants to start? Oh my God, I sound like Dr. Mike!" Sal chuckled.

Claudia began. "Well, I always wanted to go back and finish the river-rafting trip my dad and I started. My friends thought I was crazy. Why would you want to do that and risk your life again? I just had to. It had been several years since the accident. I visit my parents' graves once a month, but I really wanted to complete the trip for me and especially for my dad. That was the last trip he'd planned for us. He loved the outdoors, hiking, camping, all of it. My only consolation was that he died outside. My friends Kristy and Adam came with me. We did the whole camping, hiking, and river-rafting trip with two other couples and a guide. The trip went perfectly. No bad weather, no accidents, nothing. I know it may sound dumb, but I totally felt my dad there with me. I felt him watching over me and my friends as we shadowed the trip Dad and I had taken together years before. On the last night, I woke up around three in the morning. I got out of the tent and walked to the nearby river. I kneeled down and washed my face. The cool water hit me like a ton of bricks. It was freezing but made me feel so alive. I sat out there and watched the sunrise. It was one of the most beautiful experiences I have ever had." Claudia wiped a tear from her eye. "It was awesome, and I would like to do it again someday."

"Thanks for sharing, Claudia. That was really beautiful," I said.

Efrain patted Claudia's hand gently. Then he spoke. "After Alex's funeral, I was still really angry. I was still in disbelief he was gone and still not even sure if he'd meant to drive off that cliff. Either way, he had acted like a jerk, thinking of only himself. I was still too young to legally buy booze, so I took a few beers from my dad's stash. I drove up to the spot where Alex went off the road. I parked the car and just sat there, drinking. I decided to get out of the car as the sun began to go down. I started hurling rocks over the cliff and yelling obscenities at Alex. 'You asshole! What were you thinking? Fucking idiot.' I eventually exhausted myself and threw the empty beer bottles as far as I could over the cliff. After all of the bottles were gone, I sat down in the dirt, just weeping in the dark. About an hour went by, and I finally started to sober up. I decided I should probably head home, so I got up and tried to wipe the dirt from my clothes. My mom was going to rip me a new one for messing up my best suit. It was Alex's fault. She might give me a pass, I thought. But no, she didn't. She…"

"Efrain, your point is…?" Sal asked sweetly.

"Oh yeah, um, my point being is it felt good to go to where Alex died, get drunk, and yell obscenities at him. It didn't bring him back, obviously, but it cleared my head, made me feel a little better." Efrain took a big gulp of coffee.

"Thanks, Efrain." I smiled.

Efrain broke the silence that followed. "Anyone want to share some dessert?"

"I'm down for some dessert, but I'm not sharing," Claudia said as she picked up the menu again.

We all ordered pie, and Sal got a refill on his milkshake.

"Seriously, Sal, how do you not have diabetes?" Efrain laughed.

"This body is a machine," Sal said as he flexed his arm muscles.

"Sal, did you ever go back to New York?" I asked.

He put down his milkshake. Sal was silent for a second, like he was thinking of how to respond. I was regretting that I had asked, but then he started talking again. "We brought Jacob home and had the funeral here, but a few years ago, my niece was getting married in New York. Irene, Abraham, and Rachel were all planning on attending. It took some convincing, but I finally agreed to go. It was May; such a beautiful time to go to the city. We stayed at a hotel close to their temple. We all talked about going to Jacob's old apartment building. Abraham and Irene wanted to go, but Rachel and I were against it. It wasn't going to bring him back, and what good would it do? But the day after the wedding, we ended up going. Abraham had contacted the super, who contacted the person living there now, and they agreed to let them in. Rachel stayed downstairs. At the last minute, I decided to follow Abraham and Irene to the loft on the ninth floor. The kid that answered the door reminded me of Jacob. He had kind eyes with a welcoming smile. The way I like to remember Jacob. He said he would be back in thirty minutes.

"We walked into the loft and just looked around. I don't know what we were looking for. Signs of Jacob, maybe. Irene and Abraham began to pray. I walked over to the window and looked outside. Hundreds of people walking everywhere. Like herds of ants trying to get from one place to another. They had no idea Jacob had lived here. No idea that my grandson had died here. Life just went on like he had never existed. Then Abraham tapped me on the shoulder and asked if I was ready to go. I said I was. I looked around one last time, searching for anything that reminded me of Jacob. Nothing. We locked the door on our way out and met Rachel downstairs."

"So, were you glad you went?" Claudia asked.

"I don't know. I went there more for Irene and Abraham. I didn't really see the point. Jacob is here in my heart, not in some apartment in New York City. Irene and Abraham know that too, but I think they just wanted to see where our darling Jacob had his last moments."

"Yeah, I get that," Efrain said.

"I think that's why I want to go to the Turner Building," I said. "I just want to see what Chris saw. I was hoping I would feel closer to him there for some stupid reason."

"It's not stupid. You should go. It might help bring some closure," Claudia said. "Oh my God, now *I'm* starting to sound like Mike!" Claudia laughed, and we all joined in.

CHAPTER 18

It was a gorgeous day in early December. Outside it was chilly, but the sun was shining bright. The day felt much like the day Chris died. Today I was going to visit the rooftop where Chris took his last breath. I drove to downtown Pasadena and surprisingly found a metered parking spot right across the street from the Turner Building. I got out of my car and stopped. I just stood there looking at the beautiful old building and its surroundings. I thought about Sal's grandson. Jacob would have loved the Turner Building. The brick, the large arches, and the subtle attention to details were magnificent. I looked up toward the roof. Jesus Christ, sixteen stories was high. I envisioned Chris's body falling from the sky and hitting the pavement. I imagined the loud sound Chris made when his body collided with the concrete. People screaming and pointing at him. I started to cry, and needed to catch my breath, but I ordered myself to keep moving. Don't walk away now, Kara, I thought. Calm down. I closed my eyes and took a couple of deep breaths. I needed to do this.

I quickly put my hand in my jacket pocket to feel the comfort of Chris's key chain. I crossed the street and looked down at the sidewalk. I could see Chris's broken body. His shattered glasses, mangled hair, and broken bones were flailed out onto the sidewalk in every direction. I felt myself losing it again. Stop, I thought, you can do this. Just keep moving.

After several more times of stopping, and ordering myself to keep walking, I finally made my way to the roof entrance. I unlocked the access door with the key the detectives had found on Chris and walked cautiously to the area where I was told he had jumped.

I didn't know what I was expecting to see. Maybe Chris standing there with a big smile on his face, telling me all of this was a joke. Him there laughing with a bottle of wine and flowers, waiting for me all of this time. Chris asking me, "What took you so long, Kare? I've been here waiting for you this entire time." And then he'd kiss me, and I'd kiss him back. But no. What the hell was wrong with me, thinking Chris had been out here the whole time? What an idiot. I stood silently, waiting for his presence to come to me, or for some sort of supernatural experience or feeling to happen. Nothing. I thought about Sal and his family standing in Jacob's apartment.

I searched the roof, looking for any signs of Chris. Had he left me another note here? Had he carved our initials inside a heart somewhere? No, nothing. You would never have guessed Chris had ever been here. It was as if he had never stepped onto the ledge and willingly jumped to his death. I wondered if he had looked down the side of the building before he had jumped. Had he taken in the view? What were his last thoughts? Did he think of me? I hoped he was content before he took his final breath. I hoped he felt an ounce of beauty and freedom that he could never feel on this side of the ledge. I hoped he was at peace and felt love. The tears flowed again.

I wanted Chris so bad. I wanted him to be next to me on this damn roof, telling me a stupid joke, or testing a lecture he was going to use in class tomorrow. I removed my jacket, kicked off my flats, and climbed onto the ledge. I wanted to feel what he felt. I wanted to see the last things he saw. I steadied myself, closed my eyes, and immediately felt the wind on my face. Normally, I hated the wind, but up here it felt gentle and soothing for some reason. I heard the traffic below, but I also heard the birds chirping so clearly. I focused on the sounds of the wind and the birds. It reminded me of the beach. Maybe Chris had chosen this place because it reminded him of the beach too. It was a place of calm and pleasure for him. Knowing Chris had heard and felt these things before he died made me smile. He knew what he was doing. He was ready to leave, and this was a quiet spot in the world for him to say goodbye.

I love you, C, but I hate you for leaving me here. I hate that I'm here alone hating you. But most of all, I just miss you. I miss your smile, I miss the way you would rub my shoulders after a long day, I miss the way we would dance by the pool on hot summer nights, I miss your voice, I miss your laughter, I miss us. I miss the way I felt when you were here. I miss the person I was. I'm starting to tolerate this new person, but she's annoying and still cries all of the time. She needs to get a fucking life but can't seem to move on. She has thought about joining you and just giving it all up. What if she jumped off this ledge right now? How ironic would that be? Well, that would be a topic Mike and the group could talk about for a long time. "There were no signs of her wanting to kill herself," they'd say. "She was sad and pathetic, but she just seemed to be grieving like the rest of us poor sons of bitches. She just wasn't strong enough. Poor Kare."

I thought of Beth and my nephews. I couldn't do that to any of them. Or leave my mom. She was strong, but I didn't want her to lose a child, even though I was a thirty-eight-year-old woman. I couldn't even think about putting her through that. Or leaving Dawn. She had already been through so much, and I needed to be a godmother to Matty.

I thought back to what Mike had said about Chris not thinking rationally when he killed himself. He probably didn't have all of these little voices in his head telling him we all loved him to stop him from jumping. Chris probably felt it was his only way out. The only way for him to feel normal and lose the pain inside. I took a long, deep breath and opened my eyes. It was really beautiful up here. After a few minutes, I carefully climbed down the ledge and just stood on the roof, taking it all in. I wasn't sure exactly how long I had been there, but I watched the sun go down, and then realized Beth had probably put an APB out for me. I checked my phone, and she had called once and sent a text a few minutes ago. I smiled and texted her back that I would call her when I got home tonight. I felt content. I didn't want to leave the roof but knew I must.

"Love you, C," I said as I blew a kiss out to the big open sky.

AUTHOR BIOGRAPHY

Janelle Parmer grew up in Southern California. She earned a bachelor of arts in English from the University of California, San Bernardino, a paralegal certificate from Fullerton College, and an MBA with the School of Business from the University of Redlands. Parmer has spent most of her career working in private law firms. She enjoys spending as much time as possible with family and friends, along with traveling, reading, writing, and meeting new people. She and her husband live on Catalina Island with their beloved cat.

Made in the USA
Middletown, DE
11 October 2021

50086551R00118